LACROSSED LOVERS

A WOODLAWN COLLEGE ROMANCE

HARTLEE FINN

BRB Books

For James
Thanks for sitting across from me while I read out the whole plot.
What a pal.

ACKNOWLEDGMENTS

Lacrossed Lovers would have never have existed without the sheer force of charisma that is my writing group, Hot Cross Nuns.

It would never have been readable without the unending patience and skill of my editor, Laura.

Thank you to Gowtham for the marvelous new covers!

I did not, in fact, speed it all the way up this time.

Book 3 though, watch me!

1

Casey put his forehead against the front door of his apartment and fought to stay awake. Just the thought of knocking took more energy than he had. He tried to get his roommate's attention with telepathy, a skill he did not possess.

"What are you doing?"

Riley's voice startled the exhaustion out of Casey's brain and for a moment he thought he'd unlocked a super power. Then he saw his roommate in his periphery and remembered that Riley was working the night shift, too.

"I'm so tired I thought I'd just sleep here tonight," Casey said.

Riley frowned. The furrows in his brow peeked out underneath his black fringe. Dark circles under his eyes showed he was just as exhausted as Casey, if not more so, but he kept his composure and only showed disapproval. How was this gloomy guy so popular? Casey thought.

"How was I supposed to get in there?" Riley said, smirking. "Only thinking of yourself."

Casey laughed and took a step back. The sun had started to rise and the sky just beyond the elms that surrounded their building with pinks and oranges. He wondered how an artist might see the sunrise and the splashes of color above the trees. He wondered about one particular artist and smiled.

"This will be our last sunrise out here together," he said to Riley as he sidled up behind him and dropped his chin onto his roommate's shoulder. "Aren't you sad?"

Riley unlocked the door. "I'm happy enough to stop working overnight. And anyway, it's hard just being alone when you're always around." He slipped smoothly out from under Casey's chin and entered the dark apartment. He closed the door quietly behind him, leaving Casey alone on the front stoop.

"Aww," Casey said to himself, "so mean. This is why you don't have a girlfriend."

Casey walked to the back of the studio apartment and fell face first into his bed. Woodlawn College originally built these apartments for junior faculty and graduate students. His father had been one of the latter in his day. But the number of both had swindled in the last decade, and they switched the apartments to house junior and senior undergrads not living on campus or in one of the few fraternity houses left. Casey and Riley had been roommates since freshman year, and it was Casey that convinced Riley to join the lacrosse team with him. Now, most of their teammates lived in Sinclair House. Casey firmly believed that their closeness made them a better team all-around.

Somehow, Riley still kept himself apart from the other players with his aloofness. Even in this small studio, Riley put an overflowing bookcase between their two twin beds as a makeshift wall. It was an illusion of privacy in such a small space. Casey looked at the haphazard stacks of textbooks, horror novels, and manga knowing that each text was just another way for his friend to keep his distance.

His eyes found the brochure on his own bedside table and he picked it up. The flimsy paper showed signs of wear, and he carefully turned to the inside of the trifold. Three columns of names filled the inside of the brochure. Casey let his eyes run down each column, knowing where they'd end up. He wasn't reading the other names but just pretending to discover "Daniel Marsden, Portrait 45" at the top of the third column. He lingered on the name and, not for the first time, wondered what had come over him. He flipped the brochure over. "Woodlawn Annual Art Exhibit, May12th." May 12th, the day he fell head over heels for a guy.

"You should put that in an album or something," Riley said from the other side of the bookcase. "My mom does scrapbooking. I could get you some washi tape."

Casey shook his head and carefully put the brochure in the top drawer of his desk. He leaned back on the bed and stared up at the ceiling. His advising meeting that morning took the wind out of his sails. He wanted to change majors but the assistant dean of business argued with him, then invoked Casey's father. "I'm sure your father would not agree with this decision, Mr. Stanfield."

When the anger crept up, Casey knew it was time to end the meeting. He left the assistant dean's office with nothing accomplished. Add in afternoon practice and a shift at the convenience store, and Casey was exhausted. He didn't mind Riley poking fun. He was the only one that had a clue about the situation. The other guys had just gone along when the popular attacker on their team asked them to attend summer classes. He and Riley, though, were best friends.

"Class starts tomorrow," he said.

He heard the soft creak of Riley's bed. "And?"

Casey didn't answer right away. He folded his arms over his face. "What am I gonna do?"

He didn't realize he was waiting for an answer until it didn't come. Just as Casey was losing the battle with sleep, he heard

Riley say, in his own exhausted voice. "Do what you always do. Be the star."

The corner of Casey's mouth turned down as he thought of how he had been the "stellar student" of the College of Business. Was he really upending everyone's expectations of him for this? He saw the assistant dean's pathetic face, then his father's. Casey squeezed his eyes shut and took his memory back to May 12th and Portrait 45. With a small smile on his face, Casey Stanfield fell asleep.

2

____

Daniel Marsden silenced his phone but not before turning off the haptics. He couldn't find the strength to turn it completely off, but the vibrations from the constant text messages would surely shimmy the old smartphone off the desk. He turned the phone face down and hid it under his sketchbook. The back of his hands were covered in brown splotches from that morning's sculpture lab. He'd spent five minutes scrubbing them after class, but the damn West Virginia mud just wouldn't clear away. Daniel folded his fingers together to keep him from trying to rub off the stains. Instead, he chose to just sit on his hands and wait for the feeling to pass.

The classroom wasn't the usual layout as his other art classes. He sat near the back of a deep room with amphitheater seating. The teacher's table at the bottom was dwarfed by the large projection screen behind it. Daniel had been in a classroom like this his freshman year, calculus or something, one of those classes that everyone had to take. All semester he had the sensation of falling forward and eventually gave in and moved to sit in the front, which had the added benefit of improving his grade. With each year, he took higher-level and more specialized classes in his major, illustration and design, and the number of students in each class grew smaller. He glanced at his classmates and wondered what made Advanced Modernism suddenly popular.

Two students a few rows down caught his eye. They talked animatedly to each other, wearing matching Woodlawn sweatshirts. The blonde on the right was drawing frantically on a piece of paper, while the redhead shook his head and laughed. Other students nearby turned toward them as the redhead laughed louder and louder. These were definitely not art students. In his experience, the beginning of the semester was a time to scout out any new faces and slowly discover each one's particular medium. The Woodlawn art department was small compared to other colleges in the area, so Daniel couldn't understand why these two were here.

The door opened and Dr. Sebastian Tate walked in. "Hello," he said, waving a lazy hand to the room. He dropped a stack of papers on the desk and sighed loudly. It echoed throughout the hall, surprising the professor.

"My apologies for the late room change. We had a surge of enrollees this summer." He looked over at the two men Daniel had noticed. The redhead raised his hand and waved. The blonde nodded. Dr. Tate nodded in return, then sighed again. He picked up the papers and walked to the front of the room, handing them to the student nearest to him.

"Pass those along. Thanks." He turned up to the room. "First day of class is going to be a short one, as per usual. We'll go through the syllabus, and I'll give you the main assignment." He turned to the projector screen behind him. He stood there, looking back and forth for a moment before shrugging and turning back around.

"Well, I guess my name's easy enough to spell. My office hours are on the syllabus coming around to you now. When you have questions, just raise your hand."

Daniel felt the pull of his phone, and while Dr. Tate was busy at the front of the room, he checked again. No new messages. He relaxed for a moment, but knew that sometimes silence meant bad news. He scrolled through that morning's notifications and counted 15 new text messages from his father and two missed calls. The message preview told him all he needed and that the best course right now was to ride out the onslaught. He placed the phone face up on his thigh where only Daniel could see it. When the syllabus came to him, he absent-mindedly grabbed one and passed the rest along. He'd had Dr. Tate before and could probably recite most of the text by heart. The man obviously spent as little time on the document as he could, often copying over whole schedules from one year to the next. Daniel knew that any calendar made by this professor was not to be trusted.

He looked up just as the classroom door flew open and something large and brown fell onto the floor. Startled by the noise, he nearly stood up to see what had burst into the room— he could have sworn it was a big dog—but then remembered his phone and grabbed it before it fell. His classmates started mumbling at the new arrival, but Daniel was distracted by the new voicemail notification. His stomach knotted, and as he thought about excusing himself to check the message, Dr. Tate said loudly, "Mr. Stanfield. That was quite the late entrance."

Daniel put the phone down, forgotten. Casey Stanfield stood in front of the class, palms together as if in prayer and apologized.

"I had three alarms set, and I slept through every one of them, Dr. Tate. Won't happen again." He stood about three inches taller than the professor and was dressed much like the two other students Daniel noticed earlier. Were they all on a team? And what was with the sudden interest in modernism?

"Mr. Stanfield, considering the lengths you went to get into this class, make sure you're on time." Dr. Tate handed Casey a syllabus after smacking the top of his head with it. "Take a seat."

Casey thanked him and apologized again to the class. He caught sight of the redhead and blonde and waved, but instead of sitting next to them, he bounded up the stairs of the amphitheater seating straight toward Daniel. He could feel the presence of the athlete and his enthusiasm so much that he leaned back in his own seat, as if backing off from a fire. Casey thumped into the empty seat directly in front of him and started unpacking.

Most people knew Casey due to his prowess on the lacrosse team. The college was never an athletic powerhouse, but Casey and his teammates were part of a new age of Woodlawn Wildcats sports. The liberal arts college focused mainly on academics, but over the last few years, and under the influence of a few wealthy donors, started increasing the funding of their more competitive side. Daniel saw Casey running around campus and thought he was just another golden boy. He had those all-American looks that gave some men life on easy mode and a constantly cheery outlook. It's not that Daniel was gloomy, but his life had not been set up to be smooth sailing like Casey's and his friends. He didn't have a wealthy donor dad to pull strings. At the thought, he turned back to his phone. He sighed. No new messages.

"Hey," came a soft voice.

Daniel looked up and into the smiling face of Casey. "Mind if I sit here?"

Daniel stuttered, "Uhm. Okay...it's fine." Not really knowing how to answer. The man really did have an aura around him like a solar corona. He felt the back of his neck flush, surely from embarrassment.

"Thanks. I'm Casey," he said as he dug into his duffle bag.

"Ah, I know." Daniel said and instantly regretted it. "I'm Daniel." He didn't understand why they were introducing them-selves. It was just the first class and not nearly enough time to try to make "friends" with his classmates. Suspicion got the better of him, and he imagined a long semester of the athlete asking for help with assignments, or tests, or just not showing up at all. He wasn't good with this type of person and was already dreading this class.

"I know," Casey said.

Daniel met his gaze and understood nothing he saw there. Casey smiled wider, then turned his back on him and faced front. How did he know? Daniel was a nobody on campus, with just a few friends in his own department and his roommate. No one else would have known him at all, certainly not the star player on the lacrosse team. What was going on?

He stared at the back of Casey's neck. He had longish hair for an athlete that curled at his neck; redhead and blondie were close-cropped. He was tan, probably from running around in the sun all day, with broad shoulders. Daniel himself was pinkish and thinner, but he was no weakling. You don't carry large canvases around Woodlawn's campus all day if you're weak. But they were opposites in almost every way.

Daniel noticed a small mole just under Casey's right ear. It was a perfect circle just an inch away from his lobe. He wondered if Casey knew it was there and smiled, amused that he may know a little secret about Casey Stanfield. Only Daniel could see it, perhaps the only mark on an otherwise "perfect" person. He stared at it, enthralled, and not understanding why, he let his mind wander.

"Mr. Marsden? A word."

Daniel shook as if waking from a dream and realized he was one of the last students still sitting in the room. Somehow he'd zoned out for the whole first class, and now, Dr. Tate was calling to him from the front.

Casey was standing at the desk with him. They both were looking his way.

Daniel quickly grabbed his belongings and shoved them into his case. What the hell had happened? Did he really miss the whole lecture? Was he going to fall behind already? Or worse, did Casey notice him staring and complain? He wouldn't do that, would he? Daniel, shaking, picked up his phone. Three new messages.

"Mr. Marsden?"

"Coming," he said, shoving his phone into his pocket. He climbed down the steps toward his doom.

3

Daniel arrived just as the professor was finishing up with Casey. The man looked exhausted, and it was only the first day of class. Daniel had Tate for art history during his freshman year and remembered him to be a bit absent-minded but enthusiastic about his topic. He'd even extended his office hours for Daniel when he was having trouble keeping up that spring. Most of his classes since then had been applied arts, painting, sculpture, and figure drawing, so this was his first time seeing the professor up close in a year. As tired as he looked, he also looked happier. It's not that the man smiled, but his scowl seemed less defined.

"Ah, Mr. Marsden," Tate said as he packed up his messenger bag. "Since Mr. Stanfield here is a newcomer to the art world, I thought he could use a more experienced classmate to guide him in the final project."

Tate raised a hand when Daniel opened his mouth. Out of the corner of his eye he saw Casey watching him, smiling.

"And," the professor continued, "since he decided to sleep in on the first day---"

Casey protested "Aw, Dr. Tate, I told you I set three alarms, I'm never late, it's just--- "

"AND, AND," Tate interrupted, "Since you, Mr. Marsden, were more entranced with your phone than my introduction to the class, perhaps taking care of *this*," he pointed to Casey without looking at him, "will keep you focused on your work."

Daniel didn't know what to say. He had spent the shortened class just watching for notifications from his father. Even if he wasn't going to answer him, seeing how many and how often he texted gave Daniel a sense of his demeanor. It helped him judge if he should go back home or stay away. The texts had largely stopped in the last twenty minutes, so he thought his father had calmed down. Daniel hoped that meant he could stay on campus this weekend.

He looked at Casey, who still had that silly smile on his face. Daniel narrowed his eyes, suspicious of this wrinkle in his quiet college life.

Tate hoisted his bag and picked up his keys. "The two of you will be working as a group for the final project." He pointed at Casey again. "He's got the assignment sheet." He pointed to Daniel. "You make sure he does the work."

"Hey," Casey said.

"I expect great things from the two of you," Professor Tate said and walked out. The classroom door shut with a click that echoed in the space.

Daniel looked at the closed door. He'd dodged most of the group projects in his classes, often pairing with his roommate, Jess, or with someone unwilling to do any work. He expected that the star of the lacrosse team was one of the latter. He didn't think he'd be able to work with someone like Casey Stanfield. Their experiences were too different, and he hoped he could just put his head down and do the work. He thought he could put the guy's mind at ease.

"Look, I—"

"So," Casey said, pulling out his phone, "I have a couple of part-time jobs: one at the Front Street Market and another with a catering company, but that's pretty scattered, so shouldn't interfere with meeting up." He seemed to be scrolling through his calendar. Daniel wondered why someone like Casey had so many jobs.

"I don't have anything this Thursday, but I do have practice from 3-5. If we can meet after that, we can decide what to do and start divvying up the work." Casey held out his phone, showing Daniel his calendar app. Colorful boxes filled each day aside from a small area of white on Thursday.

Daniel blinked. "You're busy, huh?" He said it without thinking. "Ah, sorry, I—"

"A bit, but it's worth it." Casey smiled back at him, and Daniel felt there was something behind that smile he couldn't read. The phone in his pocket began to vibrate. In the empty classroom, the small thrumming was loud. Daniel purposely ignored it. He didn't have to look at his schedule anyway.

"I can't work on Saturdays," he said. "But outside of classes, I'm free, so Thursday will work." He watched Casey add another colored box to his calendar, this one red. It just said, "Daniel."

Daniel still had no idea why someone like Casey, or his two friends for that matter, were in this class or why he seemed so happy to be working with Daniel on this project. There was nothing exciting about the class or whatever the project was, but Casey seemed to be full of energy. Daniel wondered if he could feel that way one day, too.

His phone buzzed in two short bursts. This was a text message. Daniel immediately felt tired.

Casey stood there looking at his phone, then back up to Daniel. "Should we—"

The door opened and another man walked in. He looked like

another athlete, but this one was even taller, with black hair and a dark expression. The man took a few steps inside, caught sight of Daniel, and then stopped. Daniel instinctively tensed up and forced himself not to take a step back. The man gave a tight smile back. "Casey?"

"Hey!" Casey said, turning around. "Riley, hi."

"We have to get going. Diane asked us to come in early today." Riley looked from Casey to Daniel and back again.

Casey's shoulders drooped. "Sure thing." He turned back to Daniel. "Just come to the practice field Thursday before 5," he said, then put his phone away and headed to his friend. As they left, the dark-haired one, Riley, gave a small wave to Daniel as he pushed Casey out the door.

4

___

Daniel took three steps out of the arts building and froze. The late summer day had been less humid than during move-in week and the grassy quad in the center of campus was brimming with students. He'd planned to have a leisurely walk around the perimeter of the lawn to think about what to say to his father, but the midday sun had just been too attractive to the rest of the student body. He scanned the students closest to him, looking for Casey and his friend, but they seemed long gone.

He shook his head. Why was he looking for them anyway? His phone buzzed again and this time he answered it.

"Hey, Dad."

The voice on the other end was a bit higher than Daniel's and rough. He could tell the man had been crying, but the words were clear and coherent, and Daniel was relieved the man hadn't been drinking again.

"Danny. Hi! It's so good to hear your voice. Was I calling during a class?"

Daniel took the outside edge of the gravel path that wound

around the quad, trying to stay away from the joyful noise of campus. "It's fine. It's the first day so we just review the syllabus. What's up?"

"Ah," the man said and sighed. "It was a bad day today, Danny. You know the lady that your mom used to have a book club with. Well, she called and wanted to see if I'd like to join her group." He sniffed and blew his nose loudly. "She started talking about how much she missed Deliah and what a friend she'd been and, Danny, I just couldn't."

Daniel listened in silence, watching his feet as he walked. Occasionally, he would catch a glimpse of the dahlias planted by the side of the path. They'd been some of his mother's favorites because their names were similar. He blinked and took a deep breath.

"I ended up hanging up on her, and now I'm worried that the whole neighborhood will know that I've lost it." His father spat out the words as if he's been rehearsing saying them before calling. "I feel like I'm sinking sometimes."

"People understand what you're going through," Daniel said. "Grief takes hold of everyone differently, and I think she'll under-stand that."

He could hear a little hitch in his father's voice and knew that the man only had a moment or two before he started sobbing again. "If only you were here to explain, but I'm not telling you to come home. I want you to keep going with your studies."

Daniel smiled and rethought his plans to stay on campus for the whole weekend. Since he'd returned to campus this fall, his father had suffered in his loneliness. He was about to relent and go home for the weekend, when Casey's face flashed in his mind. Daniel stopped, one foot on the path, the other in the flowerbed.

What the hell?

"Has it got a hold of you yet?"

The question seemed to come from a long way away, like an

echo in a dream. Daniel looked around the quad again. In the short time, he'd progressed about a quarter way around the square. He could smell the freshly cut grass and hear a blue jay screeching at him from the branches above. Some girl laughed loudly to his left. He watched a Frisbee being inexpertly thrown by a man in a suit.

"Son?"

"Oh, sorry." Daniel looked back down at his feet, trying to concentrate on his phone.

His father asked again. "Has grief gotten a hold of you yet?"

Daniel closed his eyes. "I just show things differently, I think," he said. He shifted his weight from one foot to the other, like a little boy in need of the bathroom. He furrowed his brows and waited for a response.

"That's okay," his father said. The man's usual kind words had been tinged with a sadness that Daniel could not fully feel. His mother, whom he knew he loved, had died in May, and it seemed that only his father mourned her loss. Daniel thought he could at least mourn his inability to mourn, but it never came. The last thing he'd do is fake feelings about his mother, but he should feel *something*, shouldn't he?

"It'll come," his father continued. "Just remember that when it does, you're not alone, okay?"

Daniel smiled. Then again, like a frame surreptitiously inserted into a film, Casey Stanfield's stupidly smiling face flashed in his thoughts. He didn't understand why this person he'd only just met was suddenly showing up in his mind. Was it because he'd just recently been annoyed by him? Daniel didn't think so. Annoyance was something he usually ran from. So, why was this stranger so special?

He's not really a stranger, is he? came a little voice in his head. The one which speaks the truth.

It was his mother's voice.

Daniel sighed. "I can stay through the weekend and talk to her if you—"

His father cut him off. "No, no. It's the first week. You stay on campus. I need," and the man stopped to catch himself, obviously on the verge of tears again, "I need to be a part of this community again."

There was a long pause, and Daniel stood still, listening to the man breathe. He knew his father was pulling courage from nearly-depleted reserves.

"I need to move forward, son."

Daniel nodded. "It's okay, Dad."

"I'll see you another Saturday," his father said quietly.

"See you."

Daniel pocketed his phone. Hurried footsteps crunched on the gravel behind him, and he turned around to see Jess, his roommate, approaching.

"Hey, you have time for lunch?"

Daniel put on his most convincing smile. "Sure. I don't have anything else for an hour."

Jess patted him on the shoulder. "Good! You're buying."

"As usual," Daniel said.

They walked together toward the student union building with its cafeteria and food court. Jess regaled Daniel with his morning antics, but he paid little attention. This was typical of their friendship and one of the reasons Daniel thought Jess stuck by him every year. Jess needed an audience, and Daniel needed a shield, whether from other people or just the whole world in general, he wasn't sure.

Jess chatted the whole time while Daniel let his mind go quiet. The sun skirted behind a cloud, and the whole quad took on a muted hue, like a blue-gray watercolor wash. He could see a small group of orioles pecking for crumbs on the path ahead, each one a vibrant orange against the mottled charcoal of the path. Then as the sun passed from behind the cloud, the world exploded in brilliant color.

Moving forward doesn't mean moving away, came the little voice in his head.

Daniel blinked as light filled the world again.

5

CASEY SPENT the afternoon in a bit of a daze. He'd sleep-walked through his afternoon classes and kept glancing at his phone thinking he'd dreamed the whole episode. Yet, each time, the big red box that said Daniel sat squat on the Thursday calendar block. He'd spent so much time thinking of a way to casually "meet" him, and here he was on the brink of an actual...what? He can't call it a date, exactly. He didn't ask for a date. It's a study date, maybe. He wondered if Dr. Tate had some idea and intentionally put them together on the project. The professor wasn't the type to be too aware of his surroundings, Casey remembered. He smiled at his phone one more time and decided it was all luck.

He and Riley had a quiet lunch together. Though part of him wanted his friend to ask what was making him smile, Casey wasn't sure he was ready to share his good luck just yet. His roommate probably had a good sense that something was up. Even in his excitement, Casey grew wary. His life seemed to be shifting into another direction. Between his conversation with the assistant dean and his class with Daniel, the life he'd been heading toward felt new and unknown. He had the distinct sensation that he'd abruptly jumped off a fast-moving treadmill and was now struggling to stand on weak legs.

In the late afternoon, he settled into a cushioned chair and let the August sun warm his face. The Humanities Building atrium gave students a quiet place to study, or nap, with a grand view of the quadrangle and the southern half of campus. Casey leaned back into the deep leather and watched a group of students make their way along the path. For the first two years at Woodlawn, Casey kept his head down and focused on his business studies and lacrosse. Both were legacies of his father, a Woodlawn alumnus, but neither were great passions of his own. Casey took the path laid out for him, deciding long ago that his family knew what was best for him. He went to a good school, played well, and had a decent group of friends. He closed his eyes. Objectively, he knew he lived a privileged life.

That all changed in the spring, and like a whirlwind, Casey started spinning his old life into something else. Spending the summer with his teammates taking extra classes had been some of the best days of his life. Trying to become students of art history and theory was ridiculous and, as Dr. Tate kept saying, didn't make any damn sense. Yet, Casey was determined, and his friends had little choice but to go along. He laughed to himself as he closed his eyes, the conversations of students in between classes lulling him to sleep.

His phone beeped at him and Casey shook himself awake. The sun still warmed his face, but seemed a bit lower in the sky. The atrium had emptied out in the time he'd been napping and, as he reached for his phone, a deep hunger crept into his belly.

"Shit!" He pocketed the phone and jumped up from the comforting chair. Casey eased himself out of the glass doors, holding one open for a professor and then took off. He leapt over a low, brick wall that separated the accessible ramp from the main walkway and took off running diagonally across the quad. The lacrosse team practiced in the small field behind the student union building, and he'd already missed the first half hour of practice, not to mention dinner. As he turned from the main path into an access road that ran toward the fields, he cursed himself for not packing a protein bar in his bag that morning. He'd just been too damn anxious. And late, he remembered. He'd been late then, too.

He found Riley standing at the edge of the field talking to two other players. As he drew closer, Casey realized these were two of the freshmen joining the team this year. Their coach talked them up as exciting prospects and wanted to work them into starters their first year. As Casey drew close, he could hear Riley's annoyed voice and realized the star recruits were in trouble.

"You're not getting your sticks back until you settle down," Riley said. Two long sticks lay in the grass behind his roommate, and Casey had to stifle a laugh. He put on his serious face and approached.

"Hey, sorry I missed dinner." Casey said. "I'll get you next time."

"No problem," Riley muttered and then turned back to the shorter of the two freshmen. "I need you to go ahead and get your warm-ups done. You've both been racing each other around the pitch when you should have been introducing yourselves."

The taller freshman, Casey thought his name was Kellen, nodded and grabbed the shirt of his teammate, pulling him away. The shorter player smiled at Casey and was about to say something when Riley interrupted. "Later, Hiro. Warm up. Now."

Riley turned back to Casey. "I can't trust either one of those two to do what they're told."

Casey smiled at his friend's frustration. "Where's coach?"

Riley waved at the retreating freshmen to go farther away. "Go!" he yelled. To Casey he said, "Coach is at a seminar this week, and since we're just introducing ourselves and feeling each other out, he left practice to our captain."

Casey scanned the rest of the faces on the field. "And, where is our captain?"

"No idea," Riley said. He pulled a folded piece of paper from his sweatpants pocket. He ran a finger down a list of names, nodding each time he matched a name to a man on the field.

"Almost everyone showed up," Riley continued. "Most of them on time, too." He glanced at Casey. "Most."

Casey dropped his duffel and took off his shirt. "Yeah, yeah." He pulled out his practice sweats and began changing on the side of the field. One of his teammates whistled.

He noticed Riley watching him and he stopped, one foot in the air, his cleat in his hand. "What?"

Riley squinted. "You having a good day?"

Casey put on his cleat and smiled. "You know what? I think I am."

Riley shoved the team roster back into his pocket. "Good," he said. "Ten laps for being late."

"Noooo," Casey groaned but was already moving to the edge of the field. He started running backwards, facing Riley. "You're not the captain! You can't tell me what to do."

"Twenty laps," Riley shouted.

Casey turned around and took off running. He passed the freshman doing hamstring stretches at the top of the pitch and gave them a little salute. Only the short one smiled.

6

DANIEL ROCKED the small Formica table back and forth on its uneven legs and scowled. The smells coming from the kitchen were food-related, but the string of curse words spilling out in between the clanging of pots dampened the growling in his stomach. His roommate insisted on cooking dinner twice a week, and while he was improving, Daniel hadn't held out too much hope that Jess's version of pork-fried rice would be tempting. What he really wanted to do was sit at Gino's Pizza and eat garlic knots until he burst. He'd been preoccupied all through lunch, and afterwards, Jess made him promise to eat dinner at their apartment. Daniel had a feeling they were going to "have a talk."

The bead curtain swung aside, and Jess entered carrying two bottles of water, "How was your first sculpture class?" He sat down across the table from Daniel and squinted. "You went, right?"

Daniel nodded and took a long pull of his water. "I went. Dr. Yang is pretty hands-on, so we spent the class working first with kids' modeling clay, then some professional clay." He chuckled, remembering the gritty texture of the stuff and the way it feathered as he squeezed it into shape. "She asked us to make a representation of the grade we expected to get in the class."

His roommate raised his eyebrows and leaned back in the chair. Short for Giuseppe, Jess Morello had been friends with Daniel since middle school. Originally from southern New Jersey, his family had moved nearby during the seventh grade and upon meeting his new neighbor, took it upon himself to make Daniel his best friend. For the rest of their school days, the two had made their North Philly suburb their playground, and when it was time to go to college, Jess followed Daniel to Woodlawn.

"What did you make?" Jess asked.

"I made an Olympic Medal," Daniel said. "I thought it represented not only the amount of work I intend to put into the class, but the prestige of receiving the grade."

Jess nodded and rubbed his chin. Daniel waited.

He often thought about how they suited each other. Not in a romantic way. Jess didn't share Daniel's inclination, though he was the first one he told when he finally figured it out for himself. Jess was the trusted older brother type, and the extrovert that pulled Daniel back into the real world when he lost himself in his projects. It was as if Daniel had been gifted the exact kind of friend he needed. He often wondered what Jess got out of their friendship.

"So," Jess said. "You basically made a pancake and then slapped a story on top of it."

"Bingo." Daniel sighed. "Sculpture's not really my thing, but I need something practical this semester."

Jess stared at him a moment longer, as if considering something more. He opened his mouth, paused, then took a sip of his water.

Daniel wasn't ready to talk about the sketchbooks, and Jess didn't ask. He'd stopped sketching when his mother died. At the end of last spring semester, Jess had packed them all up for

Daniel, thinking that they'd be a source of pain. Daniel appreci-ated the effort but didn't think just seeing the notebooks, stacks of newsprint, and leather portfolios of charcoal sketches would be a source of trauma for him. He'd spent most of summer taking care of his father, anyway. Getting back to sketching and painting had been far from his mind.

His own mourning never came. No tears. Nothing. Just a numbness around his chest and a low buzzing in his head. Daniel felt stuffy all the time, like he'd always just walked out of a movie theatre. His father worried about him. Jess too seemed concerned and at times, downright delicate with him.

"It was my first time making fried rice, you know." Jess balled up a napkin and tossed it on his plate. "The videos make it look easy."

Daniel chuckled through his iced tea. The meal hadn't been terrible, but his lack of appetite may have given his friend the wrong impression.

"It was fine. I'm just preoccupied." All through dinner his mind kept going back and forth between his father's call and his upcoming meeting with Casey. The two things had nothing to do with each other aside from their weird insistence in distracting Daniel. He absent-mindedly wobbled the table back and forth with his foot. His fork slid off his half-empty plate and onto the floor.

"Seriously, what's with you?" Jess asked.

"Dad called me all through my morning class today," Daniel said. "I think I made a mistake coming back this semester."

Jess sniffed and pointed at his friend. "You can only do what you can do. He's an adult and has to take care of himself."

Daniel nodded. He knew Jess was right. He'd spent most of the summer just keeping an eye on the man while he mourned. Nearly every day, they just sat in the house, sometimes watching TV, other times just sitting across from each other not talking. At first his father kept his drinking to the evenings, passing out in the living room. When Daniel picked up a part-time job tutoring in the afternoons, he expanded into starting after lunch. Daniel finally got him to agree to counseling, and even now. he worried that he may have been too hasty to leave the man alone.

"He's not really lost anyone close to him before," Daniel explained. "He loved mom a lot."

"So did you," Jess said. "So did you, and I don't see him giving you the same room to mourn." He folded his arms and leaned back in the chair, balancing in on its back legs. "He's not a bad guy," he conceded, "but he has to—" Jess stopped and looked away.

Daniel got the message. His father had to move on, and so did he. He frowned as, again, the chipper face of Casey Stanfield flashed in his mind.

"What's that about?" Jess asked.

"What's what?"

"That face. Why are you smiling?"

Daniel straightened up. "I'm smiling?"

"Yeah. And it's creepy." Jess stood up. "Stop it." He opened the sliding glass door that led to their small balcony. The apartments didn't allow smoking on the premises, but policing this many overstressed students was futile, so the manager let them smoke outside. Jess had picked up the habit in the summer before they arrived at Woodlawn. He used it as a convenient way to end conversations.

Daniel called after him. "Hey. Do you know Casey Stanfield?"

Jess leaned back into the room, keeping the hand holding the cigarette outside. "Lacrosse team?" he asked.

Daniel nodded.

"Legacy kid, so he's probably an asshole. I think I had a class with him last year. Why?"

Daniel remembered the colorful calendar on Casey's phone.

Classes, meetings, practices were spread out like tiles on a game board. He'd seen at least two different colors that had "evening shift" written in them. He assumed each one was a different job. Do legacy kids have part-time jobs?

"Why?" Jess asked again.

"He's," Daniel started, then paused. What was he? "I'm in a group project with him. We're meeting Thursday." He tried to keep his face still and looked directly at his friend.

Jess squinted. He pulled his hand into the room and took a long drag of his cigarette, keeping his eye on Daniel. He blew the smoke out of the side of his mouth, most of it going back outside.

"Good looking guy, if I remember," Jess said and waited.

Daniel didn't breathe. "Is he?"

"You didn't notice?" Jess raised an eyebrow, the hint of a smile edging his mouth.

"Not really," Daniel said. "I was distracted, you know, with the phone." He looked away, down at his phone expecting a new notification, but it lay silent.

Jess finished his cigarette and slid the door closed. He walked past Daniel, toward his bedroom. "You've got cleaning duty."

"Yeah, yeah," Daniel said and relaxed.

"And Danny?"

Daniel looked up. Jess stood at his bedroom door, watching him. "Be careful."

Daniel's heart pounded. He felt caught like a kid with his hand in the cookie jar. He nodded, then looked away from his friend's concerned face. He gathered up the dinner plates and passed through the beaded curtain, into the chaotic mess of the kitchen.

$$7$$

___

CASEY DIDN'T NEED any of the four alarms he set for
Wednesday morning. He'd learned his lesson on Monday and was
so determined to get to the classroom ahead of Daniel that he
woke up two hours early. He spent too long drinking coffee in the
cafe on the far side of the quad. The window seat had a good view
of the center of campus. On the right sat the President's house
with the science library just beyond. On the left was the west wing
of the student union building with the Wildcat statue near the
entrance. He remembered getting his photo taken in front of old
Wilson when he toured after his early acceptance. His father had
beamed all day, walking across the campus, pointing out what
changed since his time at Woodlawn. Not everything was an
improvement in Ronald Stanfield's opinion, but that didn't spoil
his mood. His son was going to follow in his footsteps and that
started here.

He wondered how long he'd been taking that well-worn path
without thinking.

A group of first-years passed by the window. One of them had
dark hair and a sullen expression, but was too short to be Daniel.

Casey smiled at himself and sipped at his third coffee. He scanned over the wide lawn of the quadrangle and the sleepy students heading to class. He'd been people-watching since he was little, sitting with his Nana outside the market near her home. She'd calm his energy with an ice-cream cone bribe, letting her rest her arthritic knees and not have to run after her inexhaustible grandson. Casey never met any of the people she talked about, but she'd point them out, one-by-one and then lean down and whisper to him. Looking out among Woodlawn's best and brightest, he could almost hear her voice.

"Now that one, oh, he's something special."

Casey choked on his coffee and turned around, but the cafe was still empty this early in the morning. He cleared the memory out of his head and checked the time. He was still forty minutes early for class. Was he too eager? Was he being too much? Was he a stalker? He stared into his coffee cup, contemplating all the ways he could and could not be going about his friendship with Daniel all wrong. Ten minutes later someone knocked on the window and brought him back to reality.

Riley's confused face stared back at him. "You okay?" he mouthed at him through the glass.

Casey sat up straight, gave him a thumbs-up and smiled. It was a well-practiced maneuver to put the easy-Casey mask back on when the uneasy-Casey had taken hold. Riley didn't buy it for a minute. They'd known each other too long. He turned and made for the door, but Casey waved his hands.

"It's okay," he said loud enough to hear through the glass.

Riley raised an eyebrow. Casey correctly interpreted this as "Are you sure?" He nodded and waved him off.

"Go!"

Riley shrugged and made his way past the president's house toward the sciences building.

As more students piled into the cafe, Casey decided to make

his way across the quad toward the lecture hall. The mid-Atlantic humidity rose early at this time of year, and he took his time walking among the elms and maples that lined the grassy expanse of the quad. Last semester, he'd made a habit of darting across the lawn, moving like a gazelle, hopping over backpacks and picnic blankets, zig-zagging around other students. Riley told him that these antics had actually increased the turnout at their matches. In the spring semester, they'd nearly doubled their attendance from the previous year. The support had certainly helped their winning percentage, though ultimately, they came up short.

He looked up between a cluster of black walnut trees to the cloudless sky. Today's practice was going to be hot as hell.

"Yo, Casey," came a sharp voice up ahead. His teammate, Shane MacIntire, stood at the far edge of the quad waving at him. Next to him, Brett Chapman scowled at the passing students. Both men had been roped into Casey's plan to get into this art class and had sacrificed large parts of their summer for him. The two sophomore blockers formed a tight-knit unit on and off the field, their opposing personalities somehow meshing together. As he waved back and started toward them, he smiled to himself, thinking how Shane's friendliness actually covered up a hot-headed streak that sometimes caused trouble among the older players. In contrast, Brett, who looked like he was ready to fight anyone who looked at him sideways, wouldn't hurt a fly (unless that fly was passing toward his team's goal). His major complaint was getting up early. Or, on hot days, getting up at all.

Casey reached them and grabbed each one's hand in turn. "Thanks for waiting." He wanted to thank them, again, for following through with his plan and the class, but they'd already threatened to drop the class if he didn't shut up already. Neither one had any idea of Casey's ulterior motives.

"I'm not sure I'm gonna do well in this class," Brett said, yawning. They walked around a group of girls in the middle of the walkway, talking. Shane turned to look at them, but Brett just scowled again.

Casey smiled. "I think you'll do fine. You're pretty diligent with your work."

Brett shrugged. "Sure, if I'm interested, or if I have to. But..." He trailed off as they reached the door to the arts building. Dr. Sebastian Tate arrived at the same moment, and the four of them looked at each other awkwardly.

"Morning," Dr. Tate said, opening the heavy wooden door. "After you."

Shane and Brett nodded and made their way inside. Casey stopped, looking closely at his professor. "You getting enough sleep, Dr. Tate?" He asked, holding back a smirk.

Dr. Tate raised his eyebrows. "Do I look tired?"

Casey nodded. "Just a bit."

The professor sighed. "Guess I didn't get enough rest over the summer. Wonder why?" He gave Casey a sour look.

"Ah," Casey said.

"Get in there," Dr. Tate said, then smiled at the students coming toward them.

Casey did what he was told, jogging along to catch up with his teammates. He couldn't wait to get inside and bound up the steps and say "Good morning!" to Daniel. Shane held the doors open for them, and it was all Casey could do to keep himself from running. He took a moment to play cool, looking back at Brett and saying something. He laughed and turned toward his seat. The seat behind his was empty.

He counted the rows quickly, then scanned the upper part of the classroom. No Daniel.

Casey looked at the clock. Class was about to start.

"Excuse me," a young woman said, trying to get around him. He'd stopped at the foot of the stairs, blocking the other students.

He moved aside and watched the door. More students arrived,

but none of them were Daniel. Finally, Dr. Tate came in, the door clicking shut behind him. He stood behind the front desk watching Casey.

"Mr. Stanfield?" he said.

"Ah," Casey said, again. Then walked slowly up to his seat. He unpacked his bag, took out his notebook. He slouched, his stomach full of lead. Dr. Tate started his lecture, pointing out an image on the screen behind him. Casey faced the screen but only focused on the door in his periphery.

Where was he? Had he dropped the class? Did Casey scare him off? Was something wrong? Did something happen to him? All of these things ran through his head, along with, "He saw you waiting at the cafe and thought you were a stalker. He's afraid of you." His brain betrayed his calm demeanor and his face flushed. He bowed down over his notebook and scribbled whatever words from the lecture made it to his ears. With each passing minute he felt a mixture of worry and disappointment—worried that something had happened to Daniel and disappointed that he'd messed things up so quickly. His ridiculous plan to get to know him and hopefully get close to him had failed, and now, here he was, in an upper-level art class he had no business being in. Only five minutes had passed, and he already felt defeated.

Casey glanced down at Shane and Brett, loyal friends who'd come along for the ride. Both sat there carefully taking notes. He looked at the clock. Six minutes. He sighed. Maybe he could lend Daniel his notes? Maybe he was just sleeping? If he took thoughtful and careful notes, maybe Daniel would be impressed and think Casey's reliable.

He sighed. What an idiot, he thought.

He caught a word from Dr. Tate and started to write it down when the door swung open. Daniel stepped inside, breathing heavily and holding his side. He held up a hand to Dr. Tate and took a moment to catch his breath. The professor stopped his lecture and waited. When Daniel had gathered himself, he looked up and said "Sorry," and turned toward the stairs. At that moment, he must have realized the whole class was looking at him, and he turned bright red. Daniel hung his head and made his way to his seat.

Casey didn't turn to say hello. He put his hand over his mouth as if to stifle a cough, because the smile on his face would give it all away.

Ah, I'm done for, he thought. So cute.

8

——————

DANIEL KEPT his head down as he jogged up the steps. He never noticed how he avoided eye contact normally until he was doing it with intention. The last thing he needed was Casey to see him like this. Why it mattered, he wasn't sure, but his exhaustion made him less likely to wear his usual mask.

He sat down quickly and bent over, dragging his laptop and notebook out of his bag. Daniel took his time, expecting Casey to turn around and say hello. He sat up only to see Casey facing the front of his class with his hand over his mouth, as if covering a cough.

Whatever, Daniel thought. If Casey was going to ignore him, that would just be another part of this shit day. He'd spent most of the morning trying to calm down his father, who'd seemed to be heading into another depressive cycle. They'd been happening less and less over the summer and Daniel had hoped it wasn't just because he was home. Rich Marsden had raised his son to be kind and curious. When he'd shown an interest in drawing and art, he had fully encouraged him to follow his passion as far as it would go. That passion had taken him all the way to Woodlawn, and now, with the overwhelming responsibility of his mourning father's psyche, he felt that opportunity slipping away.

Dr. Tate directed attention to the screen and Daniel glanced up to see a large projection of Picasso's *Nude Descending a Staircase No. 2*. It was a typical example of Modernist art and, as Dr. Tate explained, an over-examined masterpiece. "Picasso is not a stranger to any of us," he said, looking around the room. Daniel watched him stop by Casey's teammates sitting a few rows ahead. Both nodded.

"Good," the professor continued. "When I teach the art history class, for most students, Picasso is the beginning and end of the Modernists." The next slide showed a large black square, sitting in a field of egg shell white. Shapes in the inky square appeared as the oil paint cracked over time.

"But we're past art history now. This is *Black Square* by Kazamir Malevich. A Russian artist working in the early 20th century, he attempted to popularize a new movement called Suprematism. But, since you've all got confused looks on your faces, we can guess that Mr. Malevich's attempt was in vain."

Daniel's gaze lingered on the Malevich piece as the professor continued. He'd seen it before but never projected at this size, and the sheer emptiness of the central form drew him in. Since his mother's death, so much of what had been familiar took on a muted hue. The whole summer for Daniel had been monochrome, and even the occasional trip to the museum held little enjoyment for him. The black square hung over the classroom like a cloud. He wondered if this was all his father saw when the sadness overwhelmed him.

He lowered his head, his chin nearly touching his chest as his phone buzzed again in his pocket. All morning he'd been trying to console the man, and all morning his father apologized for being so needy. More than once he'd felt that the man was holding onto Daniel just as the last remaining piece of his mother here on earth.

He'd never said as much, but Daniel felt an obligation just the same to be that representative while the man mourned. The buzzing of his phone ceased, and he let out a sigh of relief.

Daniel looked down as Casey shifted in his seat. He waited for him to turn around, but he kept his attention on the class. Good, Daniel thought, the last thing he needed was that bright face shining up at him.

On the screen, Dr. Tate had moved on to a Cubist more typical of the modernist paintings that Daniel had seen before. It was only 10 o'clock but he was already exhausted after spending the best part of his morning on the phone. Since the funeral, he felt he never had the chance to mourn his mother properly, and when he was alone, the tears wouldn't come.

Casey shifted in his seat again, and this time, turned part of the way around. But when Daniel caught his eye, Casey turned back around to face front. He was obviously overthinking due to being tired. There was no reason for Casey to peek at him when he could just talk to him normally. And, Daniel had to admit, aside from their project, there wasn't any reason for even that. It didn't do him any good to entertain any ideas about Casey Stanfield, and even if he wanted to, the last thing he needed right now was to entertain a crush. He didn't have the energy.

Dr. Tate continued with his lecture, going from slide to slide and introducing the class to the art they would be exploring in the course. Daniel let the information roll over him, imagining himself as a blank canvas thirsty for inspiration. Would there be anything that got him sketching or painting again?

When Jess had asked about his work, he'd waved it off as fatigue and stress. He'd convinced himself that it was a temporary pause, just until his father was better or just until he got back to school. Daniel assumed that when he returned to campus, the urge to draw would return. Being surrounded by the galleries on campus, involved in his theory and practical classes, would surely have an effect on him. But so far, he'd avoided the work and thereby avoided the joy that drawing brought him. He absent-mindedly sketched a cube in the margin of his notes. He colored in two of the sides and then drew two more cubes above and below. He thought back to a drafting class he took in his sopho-more year and how all throughout their first week the professor had them draw nothing but squares. Daniel returned to the habit often when thinking.

Daniel looked up and into the smiling face of Casey, who'd finally turned around in his seat. The rest of the class was gath-ering their things and heading out.

"You were pretty into what you were drawing," Casey said.

"Ah," he answered and instinctively covered up the page in his notebook. "I was just doodling."

Casey tilted his head, making Daniel think of him, not for the first time, like a big dog. "But Dr. Tate's way of talking can be a bit gloomy."

Daniel looked past Casey's shoulder to the professor at the front of the room. He was scowling at his laptop on the lectern and shaking his head.

"I'm used to him," Daniel said. "This is, I think, the fourth class I've had with him."

"Wow," Casey replied. His notebook and textbook were still spread on the desk behind him, and he was making no move to pack up. "There's not a lot of faculty in the art department, is there?"

"Well, it's one of the smaller departments," Daniel said. "I guess, coming from the business college, it would look pretty small." Daniel stopped himself from saying anything more. Had Casey told him his major? He only knew he was a business major because of what Jess had said last night.

Be careful.

"I'm not in business anymore," Casey said. He leaned back in his seat and smiled. "I switched over to sociology, though, to be honest, I'm not entirely sure what I'm doing."

The easy manner had made Daniel suspicious. He thought Casey knew exactly what he was doing. He hid his embarrassment and looked back down at his notebook. Next to the cubes was another sketch that Daniel couldn't remember making. It showed the head and shoulders of a seated figure, their back to the artist. The shoulders were wide, like an athlete's. His eyes widened, realizing what had happened. He quickly closed his notebook.

"Well," Daniel added as he hastily tossed everything into his messenger bag. "You'll figure it out." He jumped up and made his way to the stairs between the seats. Before he could get away, Casey had moved into his path. He was fast.

"We are having a practice scrimmage this afternoon," Casey said. He tilted his head again and put his hands deep into his pockets, like a little kid.

Daniel almost smiled but tried to force a frown. "Oh. Uhm." He wasn't sure what Casey meant by telling him. And he didn't know why he was blocking his way. His hand itched, and he had a sudden urge to dig out his old sketchbooks.

"Well," he managed. "Good luck?"

Casey beamed. "Thanks! But, why don't you come down to the field?"

Daniel leaned back as if threatened. "Why?"

"You could come and do some sketches of the team," Casey said. He shrugged. "I thought we could then talk about our project afterward."

They already had time set aside for the next afternoon, so why did he want to start discussing things today? Daniel tightened his grip on the bag strap. He wanted to leave, and he was getting annoyed. "We're meeting tomorrow, right?"

Casey raised his eyebrows. "Yes, but, well," he seemed to be searching the classroom for help, but they were the only ones there. Even Dr. Tate had abandoned them both.

"You have more experience with this stuff than I do, and I didn't want to come off as an idiot when we meet tomorrow." Casey quickly turned away and packed up his belongings.

"What?" Daniel asked, thoroughly confused. "You want to meet with me today, so I can help you not feel like an idiot... when you meet with me tomorrow?"

Casey returned to the stairs and held a hand out away from him, signaling that Daniel should go ahead. "Yes, it's the least you can do."

"What do you mean?" he asked. Daniel moved past him and down the stairs slowly.

"Since I took meticulous notes during class, and you seemed to do nothing but draw." Casey said.

Daniel stopped. He heard Casey stop on the step behind him. He didn't turn around. He knew in his stomach, if he turned around, he'd be lost.

"Fine," he muttered. He was too tired to argue. "I'll be there."

"Great!" Casey said and bounded past him just as the classroom door opened. His friend from the other day stood there. Casey jogged to the door. Halfway out the door, he stopped and leaned back into the room.

"You better be there," he said and disappeared into the hallway.

Be careful.

Daniel stood on the stairs, confused and a little excited. Shit.

9

———

ASH-COLORED clouds lay flat over the distant cornfield and promised an evening of thunderstorms. Casey layered his practice jersey over a thermal shirt as the wind chilled in the growing gloom. Some of the seniors were trying to convince their team captain to postpone the scrimmage, but he wouldn't budge. "Coach is at a conference for the rest of the week and when he gets back we're starting his new drills. This is the only time we'll get a chance to sort ourselves out."

The captain nodded toward Casey and Riley, who stood just behind the group of seniors. "You two lead the rest in their warm-ups. I have something to do." Doug Ballantine jogged off the field and into the side of the gym and athletic building. The remaining seniors milled about, tying their cleats or adjusting their nets, trying to avoid eye contact.

Riley sighed. "Alright, let's just do a couple of laps around the field and then sort into teams." He turned away from them and looked toward the horizon. "If we can get even 30 minutes of game time in, we'll spend the rest of the day lifting." He turned back toward the now relaxed group. "Sound good?"

A few grunted as they took off down the west side of the field. Casey, Riley, and Brett followed close, with Shane and the other sophomores close behind. One of the weird traditions of Woodlawn's Lacrosse team was the separation of the classes during warm ups. It had been like that when Casey's father attended years ago, so Casey wasn't surprised at his first practice. Riley never liked the idea and thought it messed with team cohesion.

The three juniors slowed so as not to pass one of the seniors, who was doing his best to make walking look like running. The pace frustrated Casey, but the lightness of his stride made up for it. He could feel the sophomores close behind, providing a formidable barrier between the freshmen and the rest of the team. There's no group more willing to defend tradition than these new veterans. He heard Shane admonish one of the new recruits as they tried to overtake them.

"Rookie, get back with your own year," Shane shouted. Casey realized the voice was projecting toward him and he turned just in time to see Hiro, one of the "interesting freshmen" on the team, run up alongside him.

"Hi, Casey," he said. "I'm Hiro. We met last practice." His voice was steady and strong as if he were standing still.

Casey laughed. "I remember. You know you're pissing off the sophomores."

Hiro, dark-haired and freckled, could have been mistaken for a middle-schooler, Casey thought. He only came up to Casey's shoulder but took long strides, keeping up easily. "It's a weird tradition," the freshman said. "I wanted to run next to you. So, I'm running next to you."

Riley, who'd settled in behind Casey, sped up.

The trio made their way around the northeast corner of the field. Casey slowed just enough to stay out of ear shot of the seniors. His running companions matched his pace.

"You're still new," he said to Hiro, "and it's good to learn why the rules exist before you start breaking them."

They approached the far end of the field, and Hiro started pulling forward. "I heard that you did something like this when you started," Hiro said, his breathing finally getting heavy.

Casey saw Riley disappear from his left, then pull up alongside the freshman. He put a hand on Hiro's shoulder and gently pulled him to a stop. Casey kept running, quickening his pace, as he approached the seniors. The first group slowed as they approached the start and wandered onto the field. Now, with the seniors out of the way and Casey in the lead, he let loose, pumping his arms fast and tightening his stride enough to feel his feet barely hitting the ground.

A cool breeze brushed across his legs, sending chills up his back. He smiled into the air and ran faster. He could hear Brett and Shane struggling to keep up. As he made the second turn, he felt himself pull away, his cleats digging into the turf. He saw Riley and Hiro off to the side and talking. Hiro raised a hand toward Casey, but he was past them the moment he noticed them. He reached the end of his second lap and laughed.

He raised his arm and held up three fingers for the trailing runners to see. A series of groans reached his ears, and he considered making it four.

A sunbeam peeked through for a moment and then scurried behind the storm clouds. Casey ran and felt just fine.

Hiro stood across from Casey in their scrimmage team's huddle, hopping from foot to foot. He chose the long stick and he held it behind his back and across his shoulders like he'd been born with it. Normally, shorter players picked the short stick due to leverage, but Casey noticed something while the kid was running. He seemed to have a high center of gravity, giving him much more power in his stride and swing.

Past Hiro's shoulder was the captain's team. Kellen, one of the other freshmen, stood listening intently to Doug. He could imagine what words of wisdom came from their esteemed captain, most along the lines of "toss and run, right?" Simple and effective. At least for the new guys.

They certainly had some interesting freshmen.

Casey sprinted to the sideline when the vice-captain stopped their huddle. The whole point of the scrimmage was getting the new players accustomed to the vibe of the team, so the seniors and freshman took to the field together. The storm clouds still promised a shortened game but for now, seemed content to just hover over the farmland.

Riley stood in the center of the field, acting as referee. "Play until three or lightning," he said, then blew the whistle.

Casey immediately turned away from the action and scanned the path that led from the field to the main walkway by the science building. A couple of students exited the back door of the student union on the other side of the path. They carried takeout boxes and walked fast, probably to miss the storm. He planted the end of his lacrosse stick into the grass and folded his hands on its head.

Like Hiro, he'd played the long stick at first, but found that the stronger he got, the more it slowed him down. His high school track coach was also a personal trainer and taught their team the difference between weight lifting for bulk and weight lifting for bursts of power. Casey was hooked, and his body seemed to lose some of the bulk he'd be building and almost lengthened, slimming him down in the waist and hips and filling his legs with stores of power he'd never experienced before. Not since he'd added more running to his workout did he remember the joy of running track in high school.

He leaned down, putting his chin on his hands, and pouted. Daniel should have been there by now. Casey thought he'd been charming enough to convince him to come to practice, but when it came to Daniel, his confidence wavered. The surety with which he usually moved through life shattered and self-doubt took over. He closed his eyes and just listened to the shouts and occasional whistle from the scrimmage. At least on the field, he knew what to do.

Someone tapped him on the shoulder. "Casey?" He circled his stick, keeping his chin rested on the net.

"Shouldn't you be on the field, Hiro?"

"Darren sat me out for a bit," the freshman said, his own self-doubt written all over his face.

"That's okay. I mean I'm out now, too, right?"

Hiro laughed and smoothed back his slick hair from his sweaty face. "I doubt that you need much practice. You're the best attacker in the league." He started to say something else, but closed his mouth tight.

"I'm okay. It's the rest of the team that makes it easy," Casey said. He looked over Hiro's shoulder toward the field. Riley had halted play while Shane relaced his cleats. He held a hand out towards Casey, who shrugged.

Casey returned his attention to Hiro and decided to just ask. "Why are you so interested in me?"

The boy's eyes widened, and he frowned even deeper. "It's my mom," he mumbled. "She wants us to be friends."

Casey straightened himself up and placed a hand on Hiro's shoulder. "Well, we're teammates. That's the first step. I think most of my friends are on the team."

Hiro started to say something but stopped and seemed to make a decision. "She is also in the hotel industry, like your father."

Here it comes, Casey thought.

"She is always looking for *opportunities*," Hiro said, nearly spitting out the last word. He raised his eyes toward Casey and must have been upset by his expression.

"That's not why I'm here, though," the freshman continued, his voice higher and faster now. "Kellen and I came to one of the Wildcat games last year during the Philadelphia Invitational. We really liked the way you guys played, and, we thought, since the team was on the small side, we'd have a chance to play right away."

Hiro hung his head, looking like a boy awaiting his punishment. "She only found out about your dad after I was accepted."

Casey sighed. "That explains things, I guess." Hiro looked up at him, his face crestfallen. He had to feel sorry for the kid, but he wasn't interested in helping his dad make business deals, nor the hero worship. All he was interested in was Daniel showing up.

"Casey, you're up!" Someone called from the field.

"On it," Casey answered, then slapped Hiro on the back.

"Thanks for being honest. I know a thing or two about parental influence."

Hiro couldn't look him in the eye. "I'm really sorry. I really do want to be friends."

Casey smiled and walked on to the field. "Friends do four laps around the field as punishment."

Hiro's face broke into a relieved smile. He placed his stick on the bench. "Yes!" He said and started to run.

Casey watched him make the second turn around the far goal, when out of the corner of his eye he saw something red approach. A young man, with dark hair and a lost expression walked slowly along the path to the field. He carried a large sketchbook under his right arm. He seemed to be scanning the faces of the players on the field. When he locked eyes with Casey, Daniel waved.

Casey raised his stick in the air and shouted, "Finally!"

Riley blew the whistle for play to resume.

10

———

Daniel had almost convinced himself to turn around and go back to his apartment when he finally spotted Casey. He stood out on the field, literally and figuratively. He was the only player with hair almost to his shoulders, and it stuck out at odd angles under his helmet. He waved when Casey saw him, and then made his way to a raised mound behind the bench area. He'd have a good view of the field without being in the way.

When he'd returned to his apartment after the modernism class, Daniel went straight for the closet and dug out his most recent sketch book. He'd purchased it last winter and had only started a few projects in the front pages. When his mother passed, Jess had moved it into a box with the older, fuller sketchbooks. It was never his intention to stop drawing; his hand moving across the page was as normal to him as breathing, but he'd lost the ability to see what he wanted in his mind. It was as if the light in the art room switched off.

He settled down on the grass and watched the scrimmage. He understood the basics of lacrosse, he assumed. Most games like this, like soccer, were just hockey played on grass. The particulars may be different but they all had the same gist: Two teams, alike in stature, on either side of a center line, face off and sometimes go offsides.

The offsides rule was something he once tried to understand while watching a World Cup game with his father. The man had never pushed Daniel to do any kind of sports, though he had been an athlete himself all through school. His son's preference for drawing was where he and his mother put all their enthusiasm. Yet, Rich spoke often of watching a World Cup game live when Philadelphia had been one of the venues. Daniel sat with him to watch the games every four years, and each time, Rich tried to explain all the rules. Eventually, Daniel would start sketching the players on the screen. His father never complained about doing the same thing each time. It was just what they did.

This summer was the first time they didn't watch the games. They'd talked about it as June approached, but a month before the teams took to the pitch in the opening ceremony in Johannesburg, Dahlia Marsden passed away, her husband and son by her bedside. Neither one had anything to cheer for after that.

Daniel was startled out of his memories by the whistle. The players came together in the center of the field around the tallest player, whom he recognized as Casey's friend. His eyes darted over the players once again and found Casey, who was looking right back. Daniel winced and quickly looked away.

Another player was quickly approaching him from the sidelines. Daniel panicked again.

"Are you an artist?" the young man asked. He was shorter than the others and looked too young to be in college.

"I do some sketching from time to time," Daniel said. He tightened his grip on the sketchbook.

"My sister studies art education up at the state school in Fullton. She sketches all the time. Mostly plants and trees. Sometimes a squirrel."

The player moved next to Daniel and squatted in the grass, facing the field. Play had resumed and his attention seemed rapt on the game. So when, out of the blue he asked, "what do you like to sketch?" Daniel was taken aback.

"Oh? I haven't been drawing much, really." He slid his hand along the front of the sketchbook and his finger caressed the pencil sketch of a cathedral that adorned the front. He had taken an architecture drafting class his second year at Woodlawn. And while he appreciated the technical aspect of the work and the focus on perspective that he gained, it wasn't the type of drawing he was interested in.

He flipped open the cover to the first half-finished sketch: a man in summer clothes, walking a small dog. His visitor leaned over and said, "that's pretty good. My sister would like the dog."

"Thanks." He tried to remember the moment when the sketch happened. Maybe it was when he was sitting outside Barter's Café, waiting for Jess when they went apartment shopping. Or maybe it was the time when he had decided to go clothes shopping for a summer trip. Then again, it could've been just an average summer when he walked downtown and sketched people as they went by. He always had his pad and pencils with him—2B Mitsubishis and a Strathmore—back then. He was always, always putting something down.

Before he flipped to the next page, he looked at the player next to him. "Who are you?"

The young man pulled off one of his gloves and held out his hand. "My name is Hiro Nakamura. I'm new. I just started Woodlawn this fall."

Daniel shook the hand and said, "Oh, I'm Daniel."

"Did you come to sketch the team?" Hiro asked.

"Not really. I didn't know I was gonna have my sketchbook with me."

"Why don't you sketch the team if you'd like to draw people?"

Hiro pointed to the players on the field. "We're all people." It was as if he was revealing a secret.

"True," Daniel replied because it was.

"Have you ever sketched athletes before?"

"Absolutely. I mean last—" and Daniel stopped, thoughts linking up in his memory. A large square canvas in the practical art room, a pack of reference sketches. Something about the image nagged him.

"I don't know if I should draw athletes anymore, actually," Daniel said, and looked down at the sketch of a man walking his dog. He felt himself withdraw. "I think maybe I'm going in a different direction with my work."

Hiro stared at him, frowning. Daniel felt more explanation was needed, so he pointed to the field. "Besides, they're awfully fast."

Hiro laughed and leaned backward letting his butt land in the grass. "You're funny! I'm gonna have you sketch me. I always ask my sister to do it, but she says no because I'm not a plant. And I said I could stay still like a plant. Then she said, 'You're still not a plant. You talk too much!' That's probably true."

Another young man ran over, this one taller with sandy hair and a stern expression. To Hiro he said, "They're calling for you to get back on the field. Pay attention." He looked once at Daniel and then turned back toward the field.

Daniel watched as Hiro stretched out his legs then hopped up as if he weighed nothing. "Kellen. I get there in my own time. You don't have to tell me what to do anymore."

The other player stopped. "Obviously I do. Get out here, you idiot."

Daniel watched them go, confused by the player who'd just ordered a portrait from him out of the blue. Storm clouds blacked out most of the sky to the west and he wasn't sure how much longer the rain would hold back. The rest of the practice fields were empty and only Daniel and the lacrosse team seemed to be waiting for the storm.

He flipped through the first few pages of the sketchbook. There was another person walking a much larger dog, probably drawn the same day as the last one. He flipped to another page to see a partial sketch of a young man jogging. He stared at the lines on the paper, willing a memory to emerge. Typically, he could recall where he was with each sketch, but this one felt distant, as if his experience of drawing this sketch was far away.

He looked up and saw Casey on the side of the field closest to him. His team was attacking and Casey reached up with his stick and caught a pass easily. The speed with which he moved and ducked around two other players surprised him, and before a third got in his way, Casey pretended to pass the ball laterally to one of his teammates and then skirted around one of the defending players. He raced toward the goal, and Daniel found himself holding his breath as Casey took his shot.

He missed.

Daniel laughed and looked back down at his sketch and sudden realization dawned. It was Casey he had drawn. Casey, at the end of last semester, jogging around the campus all by himself while Daniel sat at a window in the library, mindlessly sketching. Casey ran along the sideline toward the center of the field and waved at Daniel. Now here he was, his picture come to life and suddenly showing an interest in him.

Daniel dropped his chin to his chest and stared at the sketch-book. He was blushing, like a lovesick high schooler watching their boyfriend's practice. A cool breeze swirled around him and soft thunder rolled over the campus. He hesitated before flipping to the next page, expectation filling his stomach. The first rain-drops dotted the paper and Daniel closed the book quickly, protecting the figure on the next page. He knew exactly who it was anyway.

11

CASEY SHOOK the rain out of his hair. He specifically aimed it at Brett, who sat in front of him. He wanted him to leave but didn't want to say it. The covered patio at the back of the student union had been the closest place for the players to get out of the rain. Most of them had gone inside to eat, but Brett stayed outside with Casey and Daniel, somberly watching his gear get wet.

"Knock it off, ass," Brett said and pushed Casey away.

"You had plenty of time to grab your bag. Why'd you leave it?"

Brett slicked his blond hair back and wiped the rain off his face. "Dunno. I just took off."

"That lightning scared the heck out of me," Daniel offered. "It was close."

Casey turned to Daniel. He had a look of understanding on his face, a kindness that softened his features. He glanced at Brett and understood that his teammate had been scared too but didn't want to admit it. Casey leaned back and thought only about Daniel sitting next to him. So close.

"I had an uncle struck by lightning," Brett said and added nothing more.

Casey and Daniel looked at each other, eyebrows raised in anticipation.

The three of them sat quietly as the late summer thunderstorm raged on. They were deep enough under the patio roof to keep most of the spray off of them, but it didn't matter. By the time they'd all made it to safety, they were completely soaked.

Casey snuck the occasional glance at Daniel. His black hair seemed to curl up in the humid day and water dripped onto his shoulders. He held his sketchbook close to his chest as if willing it to stay dry. Casey stifled an urge to wipe the water off Daniel's forehead. He wondered what he'd do if they were alone.

"He's not dead," Brett said, continuing his story.

Daniel seemed to relax. "Well, that's good. Must be quite the story."

Casey smiled. Daniel was trying, but Brett was not the easiest nut to crack.

Again, the three of them watched the storm. Lighting struck at the far end of the farmland, suggesting the storm was moving away. Summer tended to hang in the air before the coming fall. In this part of Pennsylvania, you'd get out your autumn jackets and apple cider just in time for August humidity to return. Casey was glad their game-playing season didn't start until February, but that didn't make their off-season practice any easier.

Casey pulled at his shirt and scowled. He felt gross. A mix of sweat and rain clung to him and he desperately wanted to take off his jersey. He lifted his shirt over his stomach just as something shifted in his periphery. He stopped, an overwhelming shyness creeping in. Casey glanced quickly at Daniel who had turned his face away. The outer edge of his ear was flushed red.

Oh, Casey thought and leaned forward.

"You have to be careful," Brett continued.

Casey leaned back fast and turned toward Brett, who still had his back to them. His heart beat fast and he had the sinking feeling that he'd been caught. At what, he wasn't sure.

"Storms are no joke," Brett finished, turning around. He looked at Casey and Daniel with the serious face of a man who has seen a bit of life. Or at least, has an uncle who has.

"Lightning strikes and blammo." Brett's deadpan delivery of "blammo" gave the word more weight than it deserved. He stood up and shook the water out of his own hair in Casey's direction. "Gonna get a hoagie," he said, walking away.

Casey and Daniel looked at each other and laughed.

Casey had just decided how to start his conversation with Daniel when he heard the door to the patio open. Before he could turn around, Hiro had plunked himself down on the other side of Daniel. The freshman slurped from a large iced coffee. He leaned forward and smiled at Casey.

"Heya," Hiro said.

"What's going on?" Casey asked in the tone of "what are you doing here?"

"I like watching the storm. I grew up in Seattle, and we get rain, but not a lot of storms like this." He turned to Daniel. "You should draw the storm."

Daniel laughed and Casey felt a twinge of jealousy. This kid had been Hiro-worshipping him at the start of practice and now, all of a sudden, he's best friends with Daniel. The feeling confused him at first, not knowing what bothered him.

"Do you have any other sketches I can see?" Hiro asked.

Daniel seemed to clutch his sketchbook tighter to his chest. "Well, they're all just practice. Nothing finished."

Hiro nodded then turned his attention to Casey. "Did you see that volley I had?"

Casey leaned forward, putting his elbows on his knees and stretching his back. "Yeah, I saw a bit of it. You're still new to the long stick, right?"

Hiro's face brightened. "Yup! I think I'm gonna run with it this year." He frowned. "I'm sorry about before."

Casey waved it away. "We all gotta deal with parent stuff. Just tell your mom I'm not the networking opportunity she thought I was."

Hiro stood up. "Yeah, there's no way I'm telling her that. She'll just dig in harder and pressure me into being your roommate or something." He stretched and looked out to the soaked field. "I'll just tell her you were a real dick."

Casey raised an eyebrow and watched the freshman head back into the student union. Daniel laughed, and Casey felt butterflies in his stomach.

"Well, it's not like I haven't heard that before," Casey said.

"Really?" Daniel said.

"A place like Woodlawn has a reputation for legacy admissions. Because my dad was a big deal while he was here, people assume I'm just here as a tribute to him."

Starting his first semester, Casey felt he had to go out of his way to make people feel easy around him. Some of the other students assumed he was some dumb jock accepted because his dad was a big lacrosse star. His first semester on the Dean's List shut up most of those critics. Others, like Hiro, saw him as an opportunity to get close to the heir of a successful chain of hotels from Boston to Washington D.C. This one was harder to deflect because it required a lot more explanation, and Casey stopped explaining himself a long time ago.

Until today.

"My dad is the CEO of Winston Arms," Casey said. "For some reason, people think I'll be following in his footsteps and that getting close to me will give them an advantage."

Daniel turned toward him, listening.

"Hiro was the first one to tell me he was pressured by his mom. That's new." Casey turned around toward the windows of the student union. Hiro and Kellen sat eating with their team-mates. "Glad he was honest."

"What's Winston Arms?" Daniel asked.

The question hit Casey like a tackle to the ribs. "What?" he said. He expected Daniel to be joking, but his face only showed confusion.

"Should I know that? Sorry."

"It's an expensive hotel chain. Luxury lofts and penthouses. You've never heard of it?"

"Nope." Daniel shrugged.

"Once a week you'll see some celebrity photo of them coming out of a Winston Arms," Casey said. He felt a sudden desire to defend his father's business, but he wasn't sure why.

"Oh, I don't really follow celebrity stuff," Daniel said. "I'm sure it's a nice hotel."

Casey leaned back and laughed. "A nice hotel? Oh, I'll have to tell Dad that one."

The air around them cooled and the storm settled into a light rain. Casey never met anyone that didn't know about the Winston Arms, which, he realized, meant he didn't meet nearly enough people. Daniel watched him, a look of confusion on his face. It felt just like the first time Casey saw him, standing next to his painting in an art show last semester.

"You're..." Casey stopped. What was he thinking? What was he about to say?

You're so cute.

"Well, sorry if I'm not a rich kid like you," Daniel said, annoyed.

"No, no," Casey said quickly. He needed to get ahead of this before Daniel got offended. "Rich has nothing to do with it. It's just nice to meet someone who doesn't see my father first."

Daniel eyed him suspiciously, then smiled. Casey relaxed but felt like time was flying by.

"Look. I know you think I'm going to bail on this project, but I won't." He took a chance. "As far as I'm concerned, we're partners." He paused, letting the phrase fill his head. Casey liked the sound of it. A lot. "You can count on me."

The rain slowed to a light drizzle, giving the students the opportunity to head back to their dorms. They spilled out onto the patio, some sat down to finish their meals outside, others passed by on their way to the nearby pathway. Casey kept his eyes on Daniel.

"Alright," Daniel said, a bit louder to be heard over the other students. "Are we still meeting tomorrow?"

Casey tried to hold back his smile. "Should we get a study room at the library?"

Daniel stood up and slipped his sketchbook into his messenger bag. He tightened his grip on the strap. "Sure. I'll let you reserve it." He headed toward the stairs, side-stepping a group of girls heading into the student union.

Casey watched him until he disappeared around the corner of the building. He leaned back then felt someone take the seat next to him.

"I'm back." Hiro said. "About that volley."

Casey chuckled. "Alright." He stood and motioned for Hiro to follow him toward the field. "Show me what you got."

SMALL PUDDLES DOTTED the gravel path leading from the fields toward the main road. Daniel let the rainwater slip into his shoes as he trudged along, lost in thought. The air seemed to swell with humidity after the short storm and the hair around his face curled and brushed his cheek. He rubbed his face then clutched his bag closer to his hip. His whole mind was on the sketch pad resting inside.

He'd been able to keep it dry save for one corner. The pen and pencil sketches inside wouldn't hold up with too much moisture and as he sat on the patio, he worried that even the smallest bit of damp would ruin the pictures. Daniel shook his head, thinking back. He'd only called them practice sketches to that freshman, Hiro. Why was he so concerned with keeping them safe now?

He came to a group of students standing at a crosswalk waiting for the light to change. The main street running along the north side of campus, High Street, was filled with cars at this time of day. Most of the staff the school needed to function left at the end of the business day. It made getting from class to the dorms on the opposite side of the street an ordeal, particularly for hungry students wanting to get to the cafeteria. Daniel looked briefly at the group on the corner with him. They all seemed to glow with the untarnished hope of their first year at college. He smirked. Enjoy it while you can.

The light changed, and he followed the crowd to the other side but turned left as they went right toward the main dorms. Daniel kept his head down, keeping close to the lawns of the residential buildings and not making eye contact with anyone he passed. Old maples and walnut trees stood guard at intervals along the walk. They dripped the last remnants of the rain onto his head.

At the end of the block stood Lerner Auditorium. The school orchestra held concerts multiple times throughout the year, and the drama club produced at least one play per semester. His roommate Jess had been a dedicated member of the drama club since his high school days and on occasion, tried to convince Daniel to join. He didn't think he could act or sing and wasn't even entertaining the idea of dancing. When Jess suggested he could work in set design, Daniel reconsidered. That had been near the end of last semester. He promised to consider it for the fall, but not until he stood in front of the building did he realize his answer. Nope. There was no way he could dedicate that kind of time.

Instinctively, he put a hand on his right pocket, making sure his phone was there. It had been eerily silent all afternoon and, for the first time in a while, he'd forgotten all about his father. And his mother, he had to admit, though his heart ached at the thought. He came to the next corner and waited. Daniel shifted the bag on his shoulder and closed his eyes.

It was all so stupid, he thought to himself. In the few moments he had to himself before the storm rolled in, he'd flipped through the whole sketchbook, even making sure he hadn't skipped pages and hidden something in the back. But of the twelve sketches, the last seven seemed to be of a young man running. He ran from left to right, then right to left, moving toward the viewer and then moving away. In one, he was leaping over some undrawn object and the next he stood still, hands on his hips, looking away from the artist. The shoulders were the same, the hair a bit shorter, but Daniel had sketched enough people to recognize his model when he saw him. Only this one had modeled without consent. He'd been drawing Casey all this time in secret.

Again, he shook the annoying thoughts out of his head. He loosened the last bits of rainwater on his scalp and it slipped down his neck, making him shudder. *I'm a creep. There's no doubt about it.*

He picked up his pace and passed an old man walking his even older dog. Daniel smiled as he walked by, then remembered the man in his sketchbook. The unassuming picture had no malicious intent behind it. Out in public, on a nice spring day, he'd sketched the people drawn out by the sun. *It's what any artist would do with extra time and pencil lead. He felt no shame in drawing the old man, or the woman on the next page. Why should he feel weird about a couple sketches of Casey?*

Seven.

Sure, but taken as a group, they are obviously an extended study of human locomotion. The different angles and perspectives illustrate that Daniel was merely practicing his art. The fact that the model looked a bit like Casey didn't mean anything, really. And even if it was Casey, that just means he spent a lot of time running around campus. He probably did that for attention, Daniel thought, nodding. *Golden boy shows off his athletic skills across campus. That's it. Since he wanted to be looked at anyway, there's no reason Daniel couldn't just...*

He stopped. The rain had returned, and he sidled under an awning before a used book store. The shop front boasted a display of world literature. Daniel peered inside the window, the reflection of his face superimposed over one of the Russian classics: *The Idiot*.

Turning away from the accusation, he watched as the rain brought a steady and steely gray to the street. He thought he knew better. The last couple of times he talked to Casey, technically the only times he talked to Casey, he realized that he was different from his reputation. Casey was popular because that's what happens when you've got money and athletic prowess, so Daniel's assumptions wouldn't be too far off. But he'd seen the guy's calendar, filled to the brim with work shifts and practice. He'd watched the care he had with his teammates on the field. And while he had a suspicion that Casey's interest in him had an ulterior motive, Daniel couldn't think of what he'd want. Nothing added up.

As the rain grew stronger, he decided to wait it out inside the bookstore instead. He wanted to see if they had any books on the Modernist movement or, less likely, Kazamir Malevich, the artist whose *Black Square* had intrigued him during class. If he was going to help Casey understand their project, then he better prepare himself.

13

CASEY JOGGED up to his apartment door, dripping water with every step. Before he even got the key in the lock, the door opened, and Riley stood there looking at him.

"How are you dry?" Casey asked, hurrying inside. The feeble air conditioning in their apartment was a welcome relief to the humid air outside. The storm deposited a lot of rain as it rolled through but neglected to take any of the humidity with it. He dropped his duffle in the hallway and headed toward the bathroom, taking off his shirt.

"I took the inside route home," Riley said.

Casey leaned out of the bathroom. "What are you talking about?"

Riley picked up Casey's duffle and moved it from the hardwood floor onto the linoleum of the kitchen area. "I took the skybridge from the student union to the library and then out the side entrance through the oak-way." Riley turned back toward him in the hallway. "I just jogged from awning to awning all the way back."

Casey scowled. He'd been in a daze after leaving Daniel and didn't even think to walk down the covered path between the library and the admin building. The large old oaks made a tunnel for students to pass through to get out of most of the autumn weather. He'd just strolled along the open sidewalks, letting the rain soak him to the bone.

"You're smarter than you look," he said and smirked.

"Genius level, you mean?" Riley answered. "What did you think of practice?"

Casey left the bathroom using a towel on his hair. The a/c worked better on dry skin. He rummaged in his dresser for a clean pair of shorts and new socks.

"Shane has really improved since last year," he said. "But I think he's still holding back in his attacks. I think it may be best to keep him at defense for now."

"His size does help him there," Riley said, joining Casey.

Casey quickly changed out of his wet clothes. His body felt warm, not just from the late summer, but from all the running during practice. During the game season, he'd typically spend time in an ice bath, keeping his muscles from tightening up and easing any soreness. Today he felt light and loose. He slipped on a pair of shorts and plopped onto the edge of his bed.

"What do you think?" he asked.

Riley raised his eyebrows. "Well," he said after a pause. "I think you better shape up during practice. Those freshmen are going to be gunning for your spot next year."

Casey laughed. "Next year? I'm pretty sure Hiro wants to take my place now."

He leaned forward and worked the towel through his hair again. He'd decided to keep it long this year for no other reason than he thought it annoyed his father. Riley had a bit of that old-fashioned sentiment in him as well but had never said anything outright.

Casey bent forward, the towel covering his head. "Hey," he said. "Can I talk to you?"

"What?" Riley said, his voice sounding far away. Casey figured he'd moved to his side of the bookcase.

Casey swallowed. "There's something I'd been wanting to talk to you about, but I wasn't sure until now."

"Okay, what?" Riley sounded a bit insistent. "I gotta leave for work in a minute."

Casey took a deep breath and considered waiting until they had more time, but he didn't want Riley to worry while at work. Not that there was anything to worry about, but Riley wouldn't know that if he didn't say anything. So, he might as well just come out with it. Right?

What the hell was he thinking?

"Casey," Riley's voice sounded closer. Casey looked up and saw him peeking around the bookcase. "What?"

He went for it. "I really do like Daniel."

Riley's eyes narrowed for a moment and then relaxed. Casey held his friend's gaze and his own breath while he waited for those stoic wheels to turn. Neither man moved. They were caught in the moment of Casey's declaration of love. A car backfired outside.

"Figured," Riley said and disappeared behind the bookcase.

Casey dropped the towel and jumped up, rounding the blockade between their beds. "What do you mean 'figured'?"

Riley was sitting on his own bed, putting on a pair of black dress shoes. Typically, the shifts they worked for the caterer coincided with each other, but tonight, only Riley had a shift. He normally got extra work because of his bartending experience.

"I mean," he said, "it's not really a surprise. You're not great at hiding your feelings, you know."

Casey's eyes grew wide and for a moment he felt exposed to

the whole world. Did Daniel suspect? Did the team know? Holy heck, was he able to keep a secret at all?

"I see you all the time, so I'm pretty keyed into your moods," Riley said. His phone buzzed, and he looked down at the lock screen. Riley swore then stood. He walked past Casey, not looking at him.

He continued. "You made us all take those art classes this summer, and you've been staring at that brochure." Riley picked up his keys and wallet from the small table by the front door. "I figured you had a thing for someone in the art department, but..." He trailed off and moved toward the front door.

Casey looked at his roommate's back, his heart beating fast. "But?"

"Well, nothing, I guess," Riley said. "I'm going to be late." He opened the door, and without looking back, let it shut behind him without another word.

Casey stared at the closed door, his face contorted in confusion. "What the hell was that?" he said.

He started for the door to call after his roommate when his own phone blared out his ringtone. Casey grabbed it and sighed.

He answered. "Hey dad. What's up?"

14

CASEY SLINKED in behind a tour group and entered the main library. He was exactly one hour early for his meeting with Daniel, and he felt a little silly. He stood idly behind the prospective students and their families as they learned about the generous donations that allowed the new Turner Library to be constructed. Casey had been on this tour with his mother four years ago. His father had separated off from the group to talk to one of his old professors.

"Both Mr. and Mrs. Turner attended Woodlawn in the 1970s and met right here in the library. According to Mrs. Turner, she and her future husband studied together in the main room, as co-ed groups weren't allowed to reserve the study rooms at the time."

Casey thought the tour guide was a member of the field hockey team. Woodlawn Athletics was a tight-knit group since the teams needed to share equipment and practice fields. He scanned his memory for her name and settled on Brandice, a senior. He tried not to look like he was hiding. He failed.

Brandice caught sight of him. She raised an eyebrow when she saw him at the back of her group but kept talking.

"The main room used to be full of the long wooden tables you'd see in period films about Harvard or Yale. Those universities kept their furniture. Unfortunately for Woodlawn, the flood of 1989 damaged a large part of the main room, including those well-used tables. Fortunately, the president at that time, Thad Merrill, had the forethought to begin updating the main area to the technological workspace you see today. The Turners came along soon after and provided the funding to keep Woodlawn's libraries among top tier research colleges."

The group moved toward the elevators, but Casey held back. He remembered after the main room, they had travelled through the seemingly endless stacks of the second and third floors. It had been said that, per student, Woodlawn had a book to student ratio that rivaled even Penn in Philadelphia. As a business major, Casey had little need for mixing among the stacks, all of his research being handled easily by the library database and online searches. His new major was going to lead him in a number of new directions, and he briefly considered continuing with the tour. His phone buzzed in his pocket.

His stomach flipped as he reached for it, hoping Daniel wasn't cancelling. Casey spent too much time before classes that day picking out what to wear. He couldn't look like he was trying but didn't want to show up in his team sweats—his normal afternoon look. The more combinations he tried, the less confident he felt. Only when Riley came into the apartment did Casey settle on what he was wearing now. He wanted to look good for Daniel but didn't want to look like a fool in front of Riley.

Casey scowled at the word "Dad" on his screen. His finger hovered over the accept button for a moment, thinking at least he could use the distraction before his study date. Ah, *date*, he smiled and hit decline. If he was going to think of this as a date, the last thing he wanted was to go into it frustrated by another round of "think about your future" with his father. Casey would call back later and apologize, citing his being in the library and unable to answer the call. His father would understand, even if Casey doubted the man ever stepped foot in the building himself.

Most of the visitors squeezed into the elevator, though a few of the prospective students took the wide staircase that spiraled around the elevator shaft. With the group gone, the main room felt cavernous and more empty. He wanted an inconspicuous place to wait for Daniel. He wasn't actually hiding, but he didn't want to seem too eager. Casey sighed and slouched off to the magazine racks. A few other students sat studying at the tables there, and it gave him a good view of the bank of glass-walled study alcoves across the room. He sat down and pulled out a random notebook from his bag. With one eye on the clock, he flipped through to a page with writing on it so he could pretend to study. Something on the page caught his eye.

"Modernism in the art world marks a break from the Modern era that began before and during World War II. Despite its name, it was an art movement that reflected how the new mechanical society was deconstructing (?) man, or making man obsolete. Cub…I can't believe he's sitting right behind me. How could I get so freaking lucky? I want to turn around, but I don't want to be annoying or weird. Well, I can't help the weird part, but dammit. I have to focus on the class or I'm gonna hear it from Tate. What the hell is Brett doing over there? I'm going to have to kick his ass later. Shit, no, I'm not an ass kicker anymore, remember. I'm a gentleman. He's right behind me. I hope I'm not obvious. Can he hear my heartbeat? Shit."

The first day of class had caused more anguish and alarm in him than any time he took the field for a tournament game. Knowing that Daniel was behind him, the person he'd been quietly pursuing for months, made him feel unsure of himself and excited. He'd never been this interested in another human being outside of his close friends, and even they suffered from his tendency to be forgetful and distant. "Out of sight, out of mind," his mother always told him. As Casey got older, he made a concerted choice to stop falling into forgetfulness, particularly about the people he cared about. It was one of the reasons he wanted to room with Riley after they met. He'd never become friends so quickly with anyone, and he didn't want his best friend to grow distant because Casey was bad at keeping his head out of his own ass.

He thought back to their conversation at the apartment, and his stomach soured. Casey had worried all morning about how Riley would respond to his confession about Daniel. Would he be excited? Disgusted? This was the most unlikely. Jealous? He figured that was unlikely as well, though anxiety makes you think of every possibility. Dull acceptance was not one of the reactions Casey had envisioned, and it troubled him. Maybe he really was just late for work, and they'd talk about it more later. Or maybe it just wasn't that important to Riley at all. Their individual romantic dealings had all been brief and uneventful. Curious, once Casey thought about it closely. But the two of them had always focused on lacrosse first, then school and work second. All this time he'd assumed they were too busy for serious relationships. Perhaps Riley still felt that way.

Maybe it is jealousy, Casey thought. He glanced at the clock above the check-in desk. It was two minutes past four. Daniel was late, again. This time Casey took a moment to think. He wasn't going to fall into the same nonsense talk that plagued him at the start of their second class.

He calmly closed his notebook and stood, keeping a stoic expression on his face. Daniel wouldn't have forgotten their meeting, especially since they just talked about it yesterday.

Gathering his bag, he slid his chair back under the table and calmly crossed the room. Sure, there had been a few questionable moments when they were alone together, but he didn't get any sense that Daniel was uncomfortable.

He approached the door to Study Room C and scanned the day's reservations for his name. Casey certainly held himself back, he was sure, but the storm had given them some time alone together, granted not as much as he would have liked, and he thought it went well.

Casey shifted his bag over his shoulder and opened the door, the faint smell of old lunches and anxiety flowed out of the room. He would still work in the room, even if he was alone. He could contact Daniel and make sure he was okay, but he didn't want to come across as someone who didn't follow through on his work. As much as he was looking forward to today, if Daniel didn't show up, Casey was sure he'd have a good reason.

He stepped into the room and placed his things on the wooden table. The room held up to six people but could be reserved by just one student during the early part of the semester. Casey sat down with his back to the door and the glass wall that looked out into the library. He didn't want to watch and wait. He already felt stupid and nervous. If he sat there staring out at a Daniel-less room, he'd get absolutely nothing done.

Casey took a deep breath and pulled out his notebook. He opened to a blank page and wrote the date at the top. He stopped and stared at the vast whiteness of the paper. It didn't matter that he was being stood up. That happens to everyone eventually. What mattered is that he wouldn't get to spend the afternoon with Daniel. It left him feeling disappointed and unmotivated. He didn't like it one bit.

"What do I have to do to get you to notice me?" he said into the empty room.

"There you are," Daniel said and hurried into the room. He slid around the far side of the room and dropped his messenger bag and sketchbook on the table.

"You forgot to tell me which room we were in, and I was upstairs peering into all the ones in the quiet area."

Casey stared at him, mouth open. After a moment his brain engaged. "Oh! Sorry. I thought down here would be better. We wouldn't have to worry about talking too loud."

Daniel nodded. "That makes sense. I've only used the ones upstairs alone, so I never had to worry about that." He was out of breath, and his cheeks were red from the effort. Casey imagined Daniel running through the library desperately searching for him. He smiled.

"Phew. And I was already late, so, sorry about that. I had a phone call that ran over. Have you been waiting long?" Daniel looked at him with real concern, his blue eyes bright and searching.

"Casey?"

The sound of his own name hit him in the chest so hard that he wanted to fall sideways out of his chair. He made do with a cough. "It's fine. I only got here myself. Everything okay?"

Daniel lowered his head and seemed to consider the grain of the wood. He sat quietly for a moment, and then snapped his head back up, apparently coming to a decision.

"It's a family thing, and not that interesting."

Casey nodded. "I got some of those myself. Do you want to talk about it?"

Daniel considered him. He opened his mouth once, said nothing, and shut it again. He furrowed and unfurrowed his brows, and then screwed up his mouth. Casey delighted in watching all the emotion play out across Daniel's face. Is he always this easy to read?

"I don't really know you, but maybe that will be easier."

Casey nodded and closed his notebook. "I'm all yours," he said and meant it.

15

DANIEL WAITED to catch his breath. He'd gone up and down the stairway twice trying to find the room, and he'd started to suspect that it had all been a joke. It annoyed him that he would even think that way, especially about Casey. Why especially about him, he wondered? Just as his brain started stringing him along a negative pathway, he saw the familiar fluffy hair and broad shoulders sitting with his back to the door in room C. Daniel tried to ignore how he nearly ran to the door. Surely, that was just because he was happy his search was over.

"I was on the phone with my dad before. He's not doing well right now."

"Is he sick?" Casey asked.

Daniel shrugged. "In a way. Ever since my mom died, he's been depressed, obviously, but he's shut himself away from everyone and occasionally drinks too much. Today it sounded like he'd been drinking all day. I just wanted to calm him down and make sure he didn't try to leave the house."

"Your mom died? I'm so sorry." Casey said and moved his hand toward the middle of the table.

Daniel looked at him, confused for a moment. He ignored the hand. "Oh, yes. Thanks," he said. His father's issues had been front and center all summer, particularly when family would call to check on them. It had been a while since someone offered their condolences about his mother. She'd somehow faded into the background.

"What was her name?" Casey asked.

"Uh, Deliah," Daniel answered.

"Like the flower?"

"That's Dahlia. But—"

"I know, but it's close. We have those all around the quad." Casey smiled. "What was she like?"

Daniel grew more confused. He'd been prepared to talk about his father and his issues, not reminisce about his mother. And he certainly wasn't prepared for Casey to show any interest in her. He grew uneasy but found it difficult to stop talking.

"She was, well, I think kind is the best way to describe her. She was an elementary school teacher and librarian, so you could say she had a lot of patience. Her and Rich, he's technically my stepfather, met when I was about three, so they raised me together." Daniel struggled to pull images and information out in a proper order, one that would tell the story of his mother instead of just dumping random facts about her. He felt like he was giving a book report, not remembering the person he'd loved the most.

"So, he's really your dad then, if not *technically* your father?" Casey said. His arm stayed outstretched, reaching toward Daniel. He looked down at the veins poking through the tan skin on the back of his hand. His fingernails were clean but painfully short. He could imagine what kind of callouses were on the palm and fingers from hours of practice. Daniel wondered what holding that hand would feel like. He imagined feeling that hand on his skin.

"Rough?" he heard Casey say.

"What?" Daniel shook himself out of his daze. "What was that?"

"I said, has it been rough for him?" Casey raised his eyebrows. "Does he have anyone else to talk to?"

Daniel thought about the book club and the community center where Rich volunteered, knowing that his father had only just started easing back into his old life. He was on leave from his job, so his usual social group at the middle school was out of reach as well. Or at least Rich never reached out to them. He only ever called Daniel.

"I guess he does, but it's different. They weren't there." Daniel stopped, not knowing how much he should say. They were supposed to be having a work session, not a counseling session, and he was mindful about dumping all his problems on someone else. He only talked to Jess about things when he was prodded to the point of annoyance. He'd only just met Casey, and he didn't want to drop all his baggage at his feet.

Casey didn't say anything as Daniel rewound his own thoughts, he realized what he was thinking.

He chuckled. "I think Dad needs to talk to someone other than me. I guess he's becoming too dependent. But," Daniel paused, searching for the right words, "How do I tell him? He's already hurting enough."

"Aren't you hurting, too?" Casey asked.

Daniel lifted his head and glared at Casey. Of course he was hurting. It was his mother, and she was *gone*. Why would he even think to question that? Just because Rich was handling it worse than he was, didn't mean he was hurting any less. It just meant that, that...

"Who do you call?" Casey showed no intimidation or concern about the accusations in Daniel's stare. His eyes were soft and showed legitimate concern.

Daniel's throat caught, and he desperately fought back the

urge to break. He looked back down at the desk, trying his best to hide his struggle. "I'm okay."

Casey ignored him. "You call me!" The outstretched hand bunched into a fist and knocked twice on the table top. Daniel, startled at the change in tone, leaned back in his chair, an ancient part of his brain thinking this was aggression. But Casey had eased back into his own chair, arms wide, face welcome, a bright smile on his face.

To Daniel, it felt as if the sun had suddenly broken through the clouds.

"I mean," Casey said, slouching a bit as if embarrassed. "I'm distant enough that I don't have anything to judge you by, and, like, I may not know what you're going through exactly, but I can see you're seriously hurting."

Daniel stared, dumbfounded that this, what did Jess call him, legacy kid, all of sudden wanted to be his friend and hear his problems. What on heart happened to the world to put him in this room?

"I mean, I'm here," Casey said. A flush spread from his cheeks down to his neck, and Daniel watched this popular kid, no man, act shy. "If you want."

Daniel couldn't take it anymore. He laughed. The laughter started from somewhere deep inside his whole being and burst out. He laughed with his stomach and his brain and most of all his heart. The tears he tried so hard to hold back spilled out and ran down his cheek, but he didn't care. For the first time in months, since before his mother became sick, he felt such an impulsive wave of joy. In the few moments he could open his eyes wide enough to see, students in the outer lobby were glancing toward their study room, curious.

He leaned forward putting his forehead on the table and tried to calm down.

"Ah, you okay?" Casey said.

Daniel barely heard him. Soon his chuckles turned to hiccups and as he leaned back to wipe his cheeks, he took a good look at Casey Stanfield, legacy kid, and study partner.

"Oh, boy," Daniel said. "I needed that. I needed that so bad."

Casey's beamed. "Happy to help."

They sat there for a few moments, looking at each other. The laughter faded from Daniel, but the warmth of the outburst remained. He thought he could possibly enjoy this semester and this time working with Casey, even if it meant nothing more than a grade and a brief crush. What could it hurt? Casey seemed like a decent enough guy and even if he suspected that Daniel ended up with feelings for him, he didn't think he'd be a dick about it. He felt his own blush start at the edge of his ears and he bowed his head as if to hide it.

"Thanks. But we should get to work before they kick us out."

16

───────

CASEY TOOK the final corner around the field as he warmed up before practice. His legs felt unusually light today, and he considered doing another four laps until he heard the captain calling the team to gather around. His thigh muscles burned, and he took some marching steps to spread the warmth throughout his legs.

Riley approached the group from the other side of the field and didn't look up at Casey. He'd only nodded to him when he arrived at practice and all through warm ups hadn't made any move to speak to him. Casey didn't know what to think about Riley being anything but supportive. It frustrated him.

"I want to do some three by three scrimmages today," Doug told the group. Their captain had finally made an appearance at practice, giving the juniors a much-needed break.

"We'll swap out players after each possession. Riley and I will pick teams."

The air had cooled after the week's storms, and a slight breeze carried a sweet smell from the corn fields surrounding the campus. The sun warmed his back and his breathing slowed. Casey squatted down and picked at the grass, listening.

"Shane, you're with me," Doug said.

Riley picked. "Matt."

Casey kept his head down, thinking about his meeting with Daniel. He'd spent the rest of their time discussing the scope of their project and, at least for Casey, getting up to speed on Malevich's work. Daniel had come ready to split the workload 70-30, with himself doing the bulk of the research. Casey balked at the thought and insisted that they share the load equally. Daniel resisted at first, but he'd come around to Casey's charm and assurance that he'd hold up his end of the project. He had every intention of getting an A from Dr. Tate no matter who his partner was. With Daniel at his side, it was nearly a sure thing.

Riley and Doug got through two more rounds of picks, and Casey remained unchosen.

Doug pointed at the shorter freshman. "Hiro. You're with me."

Hiro hopped forward and stood with the other three players on his practice team. He beamed at his classmate, Kellen, who scowled back at him. Casey stood and stretched. He caught Riley's eye who looked away.

"Kellen," he said, almost in a whisper.

Casey snorted, annoyed. He turned toward the other players still waiting to be picked and was surprised to see only Dale standing with him. Dale, a senior just like Doug, had played in only one game his entire time at Woodlawn. He'd scored a goal, and even though the Wildcats were already up five points, it was a triumph for the man.

Dale looked over at Casey and shrugged.

"Casey," Doug called.

Casey shrugged back and watched Dale join Riley's team. The lightness he'd been feeling at the beginning of practice dissipated, only to be replaced by a hot lump in his belly. His annoyance at being ignored and then being overlooked made him want to grab

Riley by the shoulders and shake him. His feelings for Daniel were no reason for Riley to be upset. In fact, they weren't his business at all. He couldn't put together why he was acting like an ass.

It took three rounds of possessions before he and Riley took the field at the same time. Casey lined up across from his friend while Doug took the face-off. The captain took the ball easily from Kellen and swung around opposite of Casey. Casey started running for the opponent's goal, easily side-stepping Riley. Doug launched the ball towards him, and just as he was about to settle it gently into Casey's pocket, Riley's stick came up in front of his face and took the pass from him. Riley pivoted quickly and took off diagonally across the field, tossing the ball once to Kellen, who tossed it back as Riley passed him. They raced down toward the goal together, wanting to take a position at the goal. They were practicing without goaltenders. So, Casey sprinted into the box

Doug called out, "Hold it!" But Casey didn't pay attention. He saw Hiro approach from his right as Kellen went to take the shot into the goal. The freshman raised his stick, flicked his wrist, and tossed the ball back to Riley who was behind him. Riley jumped, taking Casey by surprise since Kellen blocked his view. He settled the ball in his pocket and then flicked it immediately over Casey's right shoulder into the goal.

Casey fell on his left side into the grass hard. Doug blew the whistle signaling a new possession and a switch out of players. Casey rolled over onto his back and glared at the sky, frustrated.

"Are you OK?" Riley said, standing over him. Casey only growled, pushed himself forward into a squat, then jumped up. "I'm fine," he answered. "Fine." He walked off the field without once looking Riley in the face.

Casey took a cool down lap around the practice field, trying to get his racing thoughts in order. Practice gave him enough distraction to keep Daniel mostly out of his thoughts, but taking the lazy turn around the southern goal, Casey felt like just running in whatever direction would lead him to Daniel.

He was replaying their talk in the library, trying to remember a clue to where Daniel's hometown was, when he heard running steps closing in. A head of black hair at the height of his shoulder appeared in his periphery, and he slowed his own pace to let Hiro catch up.

"Hey Casey," he said with ease. He wasn't the most powerful or graceful player, but the freshman had incredible stamina. Though he was steadily improving in passing, his blocking needed a lot of work. But Casey had a suspicion that Hiro would get more game time than the other freshman, simply because the kid never got tired.

"Hiro. What's up?" Casey said. Soon he saw the other freshmen, Kellen, approaching. The two seemed to be a set, and while their friendship seemed contentious at times, one was rarely without the other.

"And Kellen." Casey added. He slowed into a walk and cut across the field toward the benches. "What can I do for you?"

Hiro spoke for them both. "We were wondering if you could help us with some passes."

Kellen grunted a "hey" from behind them.

Hiro corrected himself. "OK. Could you help me with backhand passes. Kellen's always complaining."

Casey grabbed his towel off of the bench and wiped the sweat off his face and neck. Most of the team had already taken off. Only Riley, Doug, and Casey's group remained on the field. Dusk had fallen, and the pathway lights were all that lit up the practice fields. Casey pulled off his shirt and wiped the sweat off his chest and back. The air had a real chill to it, and soon they'd have to do more indoor training in preparation for spring.

"Why don't you ask Shane or Brett? "Casey asked. "They've been playing longer than I have. Since middle school I think."

"We did," Hiro said. "But they're busy with classes and stuff. And to be honest," he hesitated and turned toward Kellen, who nodded. "To be honest, you're friendly."

Casey buried his face into his work shirt and laughed. Hiro had done a complete apology tour after he tried to get in Casey's good graces at the beginning of the semester. He'd been truly sorry for trying to make "business contacts" for his mother and as far as Casey was concerned, Hiro and he probably had a lot in common when it came to family drama. He pulled off his shirt and looked at both kids. No men, he thought. How old did he feel around these two?

Hiro seemed to have the boundless energy of a young golden retriever, and Kellen... he stared at Kellen for a moment. The pair seemed like they jumped out of a manga. Hiro: short, black-haired, and full of energy; Kellen: blonde, stoic, and full of quiet competence. They made for entertaining practices when pitted against each other. Riley believed they'd be starters by next year and unbeatable by the one after that.

Casey believed his roommate's assessment without question. If there was one thing Riley did better than anyone else, it was being a great judge of character.

Casey looked over Hiro's shoulder to where Riley and Doug stood talking. Doug had kept making excuses and leaving more of the captain duties to Riley. He wanted to go over and intervene, but he had his hands full already.

"All right, and," Casey checked the time on his phone. " I have to get to work now, but I can meet you both here on Friday, right?"

Hiro jumped up and down as if he was already warming up. "Yes! What time?"

Casey lifted his duffel bag and started walking toward the main path. The freshman followed. "I don't know yet, but I'll message you tomorrow." He looked directly at Kellen "Remind me, if I forget."

Kellen nodded.

Hiro pouted, but rallied his excitement. "You promise?"

Casey waved as he jogged away, needing to break free. "I promise," he called back.

He took one more glance Riley's way, but he was preoccupied with his phone. Casey shrugged and made for the main road, running late and wondering what Daniel was doing.

17

Daniel spent a couple of moments on the front porch. He'd asked Jess to drop him off at the small coffee house in his hometown, saying he wanted to grab something for his father and take a walk. His roommate seemed skeptical since it was nearing 80 degrees and humid, not unusual for early fall, but Jess didn't argue and wished him good luck before he left for a quick visit with his friends. Daniel was grateful that Jess never complained about bringing him home occasionally, but he knew his friend was worried about how dependent Rich was becoming. If even Casey noticed his father's increased dependence, then Daniel couldn't ignore it any longer. He had a sneaking suspicion that he accepted his father's grief in order to avoid his own.

It unsettled him that Casey could see that so easily. Was he that much more in tune with other people's emotions, or was Daniel just that obvious? He'd always considered himself reserved, so it worried him that perhaps Casey saw through that. If he could see that, what else could he see?

Daniel looked at the coffee in each hand, one latte for himself and a mocha for Rich. Just as he moved to set one aside to grab the door, it opened.

"You're here!" Rich said and stepped out of the door, his arms wide.

"Hi, Dad," Daniel said, hurriedly putting his own arms out to save the coffees from getting crushed under the sheer force of the hug.

"I didn't think you'd come by this weekend. Isn't school busy for you? How are your classes? Did Jess bring you? Boy, it's hot. Come inside." Rich led Daniel into the cool darkness of the house, running through a series of questions that seemed to get the pleasantries out of the way. They moved through the central hallway, past the two front rooms, the living room on the left and the dining room on the right. Both rooms were darker than a midday sun should allow. The blinds and interior curtains were both closed, and all of the small accent lights his mother loved were off.

Daniel felt like he'd moved from a dungeon into an atrium. The kitchen and family room, which ran the full width in the back of the cape cod, was airy and light, all the windows open and overhead lights blaring. It was too bright, as if this room had to make up for the gloominess of the front rooms. Daniel blinked at the brilliance and carefully set the drinks down on the kitchen island.

"So, how are classes?" Rich asked, pulling out a chair on the other side of the island. He turned each cup to read the label and pulled the mocha closer. "Thanks." He lifted the cup as if in toast and drank.

"They are the same as always." Daniel tried to relax. The overhead lights felt like an interrogation, and he remembered his mother, happily cooking her heart out in this kitchen with only the under counter lights and the sunlight streaming in from the back yard. It had been her dream kitchen, and Rich built it himself, with a little help from Daniel, who did all the painting. The large overhead lights had been Rich's input, insisting that she may want to have extra light, but she could always keep them turned off. Deliah accepted the light but never used it herself. It spoiled the ambiance, she confessed to Daniel. "A kitchen should be soft," she'd said. "And besides, your paintings on the doors practically glow in the sunlight."

The small bunches of dahlias and lavender that he'd painted in the center panel of each cabinet door nearly disappeared in the glare of the overhead light. He could just make out the green hues of the stems, but the yellows and purples disappeared under the force of the fluorescents. His father was blinding himself to anything that might remind him of his wife.

"I didn't expect you to come home for the weekend so soon, but I'm glad you're here," Rich said. He spun the coffee cup in his hands. "The house doesn't feel like home when it's just me." The man tried to smile at Daniel, but it turned into a grimace as Rich tried to stifle a sob.

"Did you go to that book club meeting?" Daniel tried to shift the subject into something forward looking, as Casey had suggested.

His father's face lit up. "Yes. I didn't tell you. Ah, it was a little awkward, but everyone was happy to see me." Rich finally took a few sips of his cooling mocha, then grinned. "I hadn't read the book, obviously, but a couple of the girls liked it so much they pretty much told me the whole story." He laughed and Daniel caught a glimpse of the Rich from last year, easy-going and curious, ready to experience the world with his family.

Daniel kept the topic light. "What's the book for next time?"

"Something, something, by someone," he said. "I forget the details, but I think I read that one in high school."

They sat in silence for a while, sipping their coffees and trying not to blink conspicuously in the glare.

He remembered something positive. "I started sketching again." Daniel searched his bag for his sketchbook.

"I have gone back to doing action studies," he said. "Mostly athletes." He kept Casey and the team to himself for now, unsure of how he would classify their relationship. Rich had never interfered into Daniel's romantic life, what there was of it. And for the moment, he wanted to keep Casey all to himself.

Daniel shook his head. Not Casey the person, he thought, but Casey the, what, situation? Ugh.

"Really?" Rich said. "I keep forgetting Woodlawn has sports teams. It's such a prestigious school." He winked at Daniel.

"Yeah, yeah." Daniel flipped through a few pages and opened his sketchbook to the page with the two freshmen on the lacrosse team. They'd been talking and stretching on the sideline during the scrimmage, and Daniel did a quick study of them. He slid the book across the table.

"This one is quick, just to get my hand working again," Daniel explained.

"Lacrosse?" Rich asked, looking at the sketch.

Daniel nodded. He thought about seeking out the soccer team and doing some studies of them. It would make a nice Christmas present for Rich, and while also forcing Daniel outside of his comfort zone. He glanced at the sketchbook and thought about all the older sketches of Casey among the other pages. He was already far outside any zone, comfort or otherwise.

"What else you got?" Rich started flipping back through the other pages, and Daniel held his breath. He wanted to reach out and take the book away, but the smile on Rich's face prevented him. His stepfather was enjoying himself, and the last thing he wanted to do was make things awkward.

Rich laughed, flipping back and forth between a few drawings. "Definitely lacrosse," he said. "Seems like this particular player caught your eye."

Daniel felt the blush start at the edges of his ears. He imagined plunging his head into a snow drift.

"There's nothing particular about that guy," he said. "He was always running around campus when I was out sketching, and it was convenient, I guess."

The current page had a grouping of images, different poses done at different times but not large enough to be on their own pages. He didn't think all of those sketches were Casey, in fact one or two might be from a different sport altogether. But on the opposite page was a larger image that was definitely Casey.

The figure was half turned away from the viewer, in mid leap, like a deer, Daniel thought. He could remember the heat from the sun on his back as he sat in front of the student union sketching. With the light coming from behind him, the crossway and fields beyond took on the neon green glow of late spring. The sound of running feet on gravel brought his attention up from his pad in time to see Casey leap over the low stone wall that ran around the back of the science building. His lacrosse stick over his shoulders, he'd twisted to get the right angle to jump, then landed mid-stride and kept running for the field. Daniel had a vague memory of other players a short distance away, but the moment of Casey taking air blazed in his mind. He ended up missing his afternoon class that day, determined to get the image onto the page.

"This one is really good, though," Rich said and pointed to the large sketch. "You've got a real talent for capturing motion. I feel like he's going to leap out of frame."

Daniel's face grew warmer, and he sat on his hands, trying not to cover his blush like a shy child. It had been months since he and Rich had talked like this, and while his father had always been supportive of his art, this was the first time he acted like a fan.

"This is the same guy as in the painting, right?" Rich kept flipping through the sketchbook as if just making conversation, but Daniel felt the weight of the question.

"What painting?" he asked.

Rich didn't look up. "You know what painting. The one entered in the competition. The one that won."

Daniel looked at his hands. "I hadn't really talked about that."

"No, well, we had other things going on," Rich said. There was a small tremor in his voice, but the man held strong. "Looking at this sketchbook makes me sad."

Daniel reached up instinctively to pull them away, but Rich kept turning the pages.

"We never got a chance to celebrate you and your work," he said. The man sat up and leaned back in his chair abruptly, startling Daniel. A few tears streamed from the corners of his stepfather's eyes. The man smiled.

"Sorry. I didn't want to cry on your sketchbook." He chuckled and wiped his tears. "I'm turning into a silly old man, aren't I?"

Daniel nodded. "But, well, that's not entirely a bad thing, I guess." He thought of Casey, sitting across from him in the study room like a ball of sunshine in human form. Just a few moments with him and he'd felt better, even optimistic. Could he be like that for someone else? Could he be like that now?

"Well, I don't know if you're *turning* so much as entering into your final form."

Rich looked up and raised an eyebrow. Daniel stared back, waiting. Had he gone too far and spoiled the moment? He wasn't cut out for this.

Rich bent forward and laughed. It was a deep, hearty laugh, unconsciously and genuinely given. To Daniel, it sounded like Christmas from long ago when their family was three and the future was certain. He started laughing himself, mostly to keep from crying.

Rich coughed and in between laughs said, "you sound just like your mother."

Daniel's "sorry" was instant and quiet.

"Never," said Rich, his laughter slowing but his smile still lighting up his face. "Never be sorry for reminding me or you or anyone of her." He reached out and grabbed Daniel's hands. "She's the best of both of us. Always."

Daniel nodded and bowed his head letting a few tears fall into his lap.

18

DANIEL SAT on the porch swing thinking. The rest of the afternoon with his father had been easy, comfortable, and they had a chance to talk about things that had always been put to the side when they were together. Daniel talked about his classes, and Rich talked about his job. Daniel asked about the Thanksgiving holiday, and Rich suggested they go out to a restaurant. The kind of conversations that families typically have when things are just going along normally. For Daniel, it felt like a dream.

As he sat on the front porch, waiting for Jess to pick him up and take him back to campus, he realized he had one person to thank for this dream like afternoon: Casey Stanfield. Daniel shook his head and was amazed that somebody like Casey not only had popped into his life so dramatically but had given him some of the best advice he'd ever received.

What possessed this guy, this guy so full of life and energy, so opposite of who Daniel was, to latch on to him in the way that he had? Why was he so interested and why did he take the time to help Daniel in his relationship? A small part of him deep down had inklings, maybe even hopes, that Casey had some sort of deeper interest in Daniel. But he was full of doubt, and experience made sure that those possibilities didn't linger long. It's not that Daniel didn't like himself, but if anything, he was self aware. And he was all too aware of not being in the same league as Casey.

His phone buzzed and he checked the screen, only to see an alert for storms later that day. He thought about calling Casey to tell him how well the afternoon went and thanking him for his advice. Would that make sense? Would it be weird to call Casey out of the blue on a weekend when he's probably out enjoying himself? He would probably be bothering him. Did they have the kind of relationship where they called each other?

Daniel leaned back in the rocker and stared up at the wooden roof of the porch. Why is everything so complicated? For the first time in months, a cloud of grief had lifted while he was at home and he felt calm. The air cooled in anticipation of the storm to come, and a slight breeze chilled him as he sat on the porch. It swept the stale late summer air away. It felt like a fresh start.

Looking at his phone Daniel figured a text message would be appropriate. If a phone call was too intimate then a text message should be perfect for a friend, especially a new friend. Casey had invariably helped him. His advice had carried Daniel through what could've been an awkward and painful conversation. But he steered their meeting toward laughter, toward looking forward, almost precisely what Casey had said. He was so grateful for that moment. Had Casey been in the room, he probably would've rushed over and hugged him.

He felt a warmth in his chest at the thought, and his thumb slipped from the message button to the call button on Casey's contact screen. Daniel heard the ringing and knowing that hanging up would only make things worse, he quickly put the phone to his face and cringed.

Casey answered immediately. "Hey! Hi!"

Daniel stuttered. "Hi. Am I, am I bothering you, Casey? It's Daniel." He died a little inside.

"Yeah, I know it's you. What's up? Everything OK? Can I help? Where are you?" Casey rattled off questions just like his father had when he arrived.

"I'm at home actually and everything is really fine. I just wanted to tell you that I took your advice." He didn't know how to thank someone without sounding creepy. When did he start worrying that thanking people was creepy?

"Really? Awesome! What happened?" Casey said. He was out of breath, and Daniel wondered if he had called him in the middle of practice.

"Are you running right now? Are you at practice?"

Casey laughed. "No, no. Actually, I'm on my way to work. Practice just ended. Tell me what happened? What made my advice so wonderful?"

Daniel could picture the smirk on Casey's face, and it kind of annoyed him. But also, there was part of him that wished he could see it in person. "I just tried to keep us looking forward, like you said. And at one point, I even made him laugh." Daniel's voice got quiet as the weight of the situation swept over him. "I can't remember the last time my stepfather laughed. It is such a good sound."

Casey was silent for a moment, and Daniel wondered if he had lost the connection. He was about to ask if he was still there when Casey said, "I am so glad. That's amazing! You guys deserve to laugh."

Daniel held the phone close to the side of his face, almost wishing he could pass through it and give Casey the hug that scared him to think about. He bent forward, closed his eyes and willed himself not to cry, at least not while he was on the phone. This man had entered his life and changed it in ways that he couldn't even imagine. What changes were coming for him?

Where in the hell was this going to go? More importantly, where did he want it to go?

"Look, I want nothing more than to talk to you about this, but I'll have to wait until you come back. I'm already late for work."

"Ah," Daniel said. "I'm sorry. I get it. I'm holding you up."

Neither one of them said anything for a moment, and Daniel got the impression that Casey was now uncomfortable. He looked for a way to end the phone call without making things more awkward.

"I guess I will see you –"

"You and I are going to hang out after class on Monday, got it?" Casey said "I gotta go, but I'm not gonna go without you telling me we're gonna hang out Monday after class, right?"

Daniel sat back up, surprised. "Hang out?"

"Yeah," Casey said, out of breath again. It sounded like he had started running "You and me, with you telling me exactly what happened today. If I was so helpful, I want you to tell me how great I am in person."

Daniel laughed. He couldn't help it. Casey was too much. To anyone else it would've seemed like an egotistical comment, maybe even out of place considering the gravity of Daniel and Rich's situation. But from Casey, it made sense because he had been helpful, he had been kind, and at this moment, there is no one in the world that Daniel wanted to talk to you more than him.

"You got it," Daniel said, smiling wide. Without thinking, he added, "it's a date.""

Daniel froze, hearing only the sound of running footsteps on the other end of the phone. Maybe Casey hadn't heard him, maybe he had leapt over a fire hydrant or something and didn't hear the word "date" come out of his mouth. Maybe there's a way that he can backtrack and say "Just kidding, really."

"Yeah," Casey said. "It *is* a date. Monday. Gotta go."

Casey hung up. Daniel held the phone away from his face and looked at it as if it had bitten his ear. Surely, he was just kidding, Daniel thought. They were just gonna hang out after class, something they've done since the beginning of the semester, though not by Daniel's choice at first. Wasn't that the thing, Daniel thought. At first, he didn't want to hang out with him or work with him on a project. At first, he didn't see Casey clearly. But now? Now what?

He was still staring at his phone when Jess stepped onto the porch. "Are you OK?"

Daniel nodded. "Maybe?"

Jess squinted and frowned. "Lacrosse?"

"What?"

Jess took a few steps back and lit a cigarette. "Never mind. Let me just have this, and then we'll head back to campus." He paused, took a long drag from his cigarette and muttered. "I'm sure you're eager to get back."

19

———————

CASEY TOOK his time walking down the street, enjoying the coolness of the night. His coworkers asked him to go out for drinks, but between a long practice and a particularly busy shift at the store, all he wanted was to get home and close his eyes. But he had a good mile and a half before he got to his apartment, and while his body was weary, his spirit was high and carried him along.

He had heard the word immediately, and it filled his brain, like one of those word clouds he'd seen online. Date. Date. Date. Date. And he hadn't even been the one to say it, Daniel had. Daniel said it was a date. Daniel said date. Date with Daniel.

Date.

When he had heard the word, he started running faster to give himself time to make sure he wasn't hearing things. But the store had been just around the corner, and he took a chance. "Yes, it is a date." And he hung up before Daniel could contradict.

Casey searched the night sky for signs it was a dirty trick. But he didn't care because, as far as he was concerned, he had a date with Daniel, and he was gonna make the most of it. And the best part? Daniel knew it was a date. He had no idea what he was gonna wear, but since it was after class, it didn't matter. He needed to let Riley know he wouldn't be at practice that day.

Just as he was about to make the left onto Elm, the devil himself appeared out of the darkness. Riley approached the intersection from the opposite way and stopped when he recognized Casey. They hadn't had a conversation since Casey told him about his feelings for Daniel. The moment he saw his face, he remembered how confused and upset he was. Riley had avoided him during practice, so he wasn't sure how to approach him now. And then he remembered he had a date with Daniel. All would be right with the world.

Casey smiled and waved. "Riley, yo, let's walk together"

Riley looked up from his phone and saw Casey and seemed relieved. "Yeah, OK," and put his phone into his back pocket.

They walked together in silence for half a block, Casey trying to get a feel for his friend's mood, but to his surprise, it was Riley that broke the silence.

"Sorry for being a dick earlier today."

Casey kept walking. "Hadn't noticed." He smiled.

"I noticed. And that's all that matters. And I'm sorry."

For Casey, this seems to have settled things, but his excitement tended to make his mouth run. "So, guess what? Wait. Don't guess. I've got a date with Daniel on Monday."

Riley laughed and turned to his friend. "Is it technically a date or is that just how you're thinking of it?"

Casey pointed at Riley "I'll have you know that I'm not the one that called it a date. Daniel said it's a date."

Riley stopped walking and turned back toward his friend, shaking his head. "You know what? I'm not gonna burst your bubble. Congratulations." He stood there smiling, waiting for Casey to catch up to him and then added, "So what are you gonna wear?"

Casey grinned. He knew Riley asked the question because he knew how much it would preoccupy Casey on the day. To avoid being teased by his roommate, he was seriously considering just wearing his team sweats and not caring. But a little bit of teasing was worth it to look good for Daniel on their date. He kept rolling the word around in his head until he fell a hand on his shoulder, pushing him sideways.

"You have the stupidest grin on your face," Riley said. "I'm happy for you. Honestly"

Casey felt such deep appreciation for his friend. He and Riley had only known each other for a few years, but their immediate friendship had meant the world to him. They came from very different backgrounds, but Riley was always a calming presence in his life. Riley was the moon to Casey's sun, one of the past players told them. They immediately made a good pair when they joined the lacrosse team. He could see a lot of that early rapport in Hiro and Kellen this year.

"You talk to your dad lately," Riley asked.

Casey's mood chilled a bit. "Yesterday, after you left."

Riley seemed to wait for an answer. They walked along the final block on Elm in silence.

"He was asking about the holiday coming up," Casey said. "Making sure that I was coming home."

Riley's phone buzzed, but he ignored it. "Are you going home?"

Casey didn't care for the change of subject. "Probably. He said he wants to talk about school and the changes I'm making." Casey held up his hands and did air quotes for the word changes. "I don't know where that conversation is gonna go, but I do know it's not one that I want to have."

The cool air dampened his mood. His stomach still felt warm, full of hot butterflies, and while he liked the feeling of anticipation, he also feared the anxiety that could accompany it. Now, discussing his father with Riley, that anxiety started to perk up and what had been a pleasant feeling turned to frustration.

"You don't need me to tell you he's not gonna be happy." They reached their apartment building and lowered their voices as they approached. "But, he's not gonna be happy."

Casey led the way up the stairs. "Oh, I know. I could sense his frustration, but at least I can say he's not paying. So, he doesn't get to tell me what to do."

"He can still try," Riley said.

The moment they reached their apartment door, weariness took over Casey, and whether it was the change in topic or just the weight of the day, all Casey wanted was to be faced down in his mattress.

"He'll try. But it won't matter," Casey said and yawned. "You know why it won't matter?"

Riley unlocked the door. "Why?"

Casey leaned in close to his roommate, "Cause I have a date with Daniel."

20

THE STORMS over the weekend seemed to have broken through most of the mid-autumn heat. Daniel enjoyed the crisp morning air and used that as the excuse of why he was arriving at his modernism class so early. So early, in fact, that he was the first student in the lecture hall. He wondered if he had gotten the day wrong. He checked his phone, but he was right. It was indeed Monday. The Monday of his date with Casey.

Why did he have to call it a date? It was just a saying, just a figure of speech. And now he's filled with all of these anxieties and emotions that he wasn't expecting. Or maybe he was expecting them but didn't want to feel them. It had been a hurtful year for Daniel in so many ways, and the last thing he needed was to be hurt again.

Resigned to his fate, he slowly trudged up the stairs to his table and unpacked his things. He pulled his sketchbook closer and flipped open to a blank page. He unwrapped his pencil holder, pulled out a medium hardness pencil, and started sketching absentmindedly. Part of him wanted to do a quick study of the front of the lecture hall. He thought refreshing his drafting skills would make him more prone to do more than simple backgrounds for his models. The sharp lines and contrast between the blackboard and the white wall, the rolled-up projector screen hanging above it all would make an interesting little scene. The wide-open areas of the wall made the viewer want to add things to the image.

As he sketched the boundaries of the blackboard, he wondered if he was actually sketching a little bit of himself. Is that what Casey saw when he looked at him and why he's so interested in him? Did he see something that was empty and that he desperately... Daniel's mind started to wander into places it hadn't been for a while, and as his face flushed, he started considering that even the phrasing of his thoughts could be suggestive.

The door opened and a couple of the other students walked in. They took no notice of Daniel, which he was used to. Usually with his head bent down, leaning over a sketchbook, he wasn't one to notice even when he was noticed. But anticipating the arrival of Casey had him on edge, and he understood that his nervousness was actually excitement. He had to admit, maybe part of him wanted to say the word date because the rest of him was really looking forward to today.

Why had he gotten to class so early? He had a feeling it was going to be an endless wait.

Casey finally arrived three minutes to class time and bounded up the stairs. Daniel was always fascinated by his agility, which was why he found himself sketching him so often. At first, he didn't even know Casey. He was just this blur of movement, always in his periphery. Jess would say it's the legacy kid living the easy life, but Daniel was starting to understand that wasn't actually the case. Casey wasn't running through life as if the way had been paved for him. And if he thought closely, he realized Casey was probably running away from that paved path.

He gave Casey a searching look. Casey sat down and swiveled in his seat to face him. "Something on my face?"

"You seem extra energetic this morning," Daniel said, holding back what he was actually thinking.

Casey smiled broadly in that welcoming way that was the opposite of the lecture hall sketch. It wasn't a place that you wanted to fill, but it was the place that filled you. Daniel never knew a smile could make him feel whole. He looked away, starting to understand the dangerous territory he was in.

"It's cool outside," Casey said. "I seem to thrive more in the cooler months."

Daniel looked back in case he seemed to be avoiding him. There was no doubt in Casey's face but a small note of concern. His eyebrows started to furrow gently, and Daniel's immediate response was to assuage the man's feelings. The last thing he wanted was Casey to be unhappy.

"Good," Daniel said, mustering all of his reserves of cheerfulness. "So, what are we gonna do today?" He hid his shaking hands under the desk, gripping the pencil so tight he almost broke it in half. "I don't have another class until late afternoon, but I do want to thank you."

Casey's smile brightened again. "We can do anything you want," he said. "And I don't know what you want to thank me for, but I'll take it." He held Daniel's gaze for a second longer than he was comfortable, but he couldn't find the strength to break away. Over Casey's shoulder, he saw one of his teammates, the redhead, jogging up the stairs toward them. Deep down, he was relieved for the distraction. He really had no idea how to handle Casey.

"Casey, have you seen the freshman yet today?" Shane said. He looked briefly at Daniel and nodded in recognition. Daniel smiled in response, feeling included. It was a strange feeling. He was used to being ignored or seen in the background of other groups. But the redhead had noticed him as a friend of Casey's and therefore worthy of his acknowledgment.

"No. Not this morning, but I don't know if they have early classes. What's up?"

Shane took off his backpack and squatted on the small landing. He sighed. "The captain was asking me about it this morning." He waved off Casey's unspoken comment.

"I know, I know. The captain was actually doing captain stuff. Well, to be honest, he was pushing captain stuff on me, and I'm supposed to find these two and get them to the athletic liaison." Shane shook his head, and Daniel had the impression that administrative tasks were not his strong suit.

"Where is Riley? He's usually doing all the captain stuff for the captain?" Casey asked.

Shane just shrugged. He looked up at the wall clock in the room. "I don't know. Prof is late though. How long do we have to wait before we can leave?"

It was Casey's turn to shrug. "Ten minutes?" He turned back to Daniel. "I'll wait for however long it takes."

Daniel felt that in his stomach, a warm sensation that seemed to wrap his insides around each other. He wasn't sure if Casey meant anything by that statement, and Daniel knew he could misunderstand. Daniel knew he wanted to misunderstand. Casey looked away as Shane took his seat and for a moment, Daniel hoped he wouldn't look back. He needed a moment to get his composure back to be the reserved Daniel. He needed to stop being attracted to Casey Stanfield.

He was in so much trouble.

The door slammed open three minutes after class was supposed to start and Professor Tate hurried in. He had a stack of paper in one arm and his messenger bag seemed ready to fall off of his other. He slammed everything down on the front desk, took two deep breaths, and then looked up at the class.

"I would like to say for the record that I am late because of the Dean of the College of Business, who is in the habit of harassing me. I would also like to state for the record that the festivities to welcome the new president at Woodlawn College are a major pain in the ass for me personally. As is the aforementioned Dean of the College of Business."

He looked at his class waiting for an answer. Daniel only felt confusion, but Casey laughed. Daniel wondered if he knew something that he didn't.

Professor Tate busied himself getting his lecture slides ready. The murmuring among the students had settled down as Tate dimmed the lecture hall lights from a control panel on the podium.

"Oh, before I forget. Mr. Marsden. See me after class."

Daniel sat up in his chair after being called out. He was about to call out in response, but Tate had turned to his slides and started lecturing.

Casey half turned toward him and leaned back in his chair. "You in trouble?"

Daniel whispered. "I have no idea."

Casey nodded and Daniel noted the way the curls in his hair moved against the back of his neck.

"I'll wait for you." Casey said. "I mean it. I'll wait."

So much trouble.

21

CASEY SAT on the edge of the stone wall outside the arts building and pouted. Professor Tate had kidnapped Daniel and, as far as he was concerned, was holding him hostage just to make Casey miserable. Today was the day of their date, he thought, and Tate was making a pest of himself. He was starting to get frustrated as the groups of students filtered into their classes, emptying out the quad for the next period. He had to take action, and suddenly a solution arrived.

"Hi Casey, what are you doing here?" Derek Morton, Dean of the College of Business approached him, hands in his pockets and a smirk on his face.

"Sulking," said Casey. He wasted no time calling in a favor. "Can you go rescue my friend from Professor Tate please, Dean Morton."

The dean looked from Casey back to the doors of the art building and then back to Casey. "Well, I'm here to pick up the professor so I guess I can speed things along." He took a few steps towards the door and then turned back. "That all you need?"

"Yep, I'm good. Go get 'em." Casey said and waved the dean

away. Had it been any other member of the administration, Casey would have been courteous and not so familiar. However, he and the dean had worked together, so to speak, over the summer and the time for formalities had long passed.

Derek nodded and disappeared behind the large oak doors.

Moments later Daniel emerged, the sound of Professor Tate's raised voice following him. He caught sight of Casey and joined him at the wall. "He's not yelling after me," Daniel said. "The moment the Dean walked in and started yelling at him, I basically had to get away."

Casey smiled. "You're welcome." He hopped down off the wall and forced himself not to take Daniel's arm. "Let's go."

Daniel adjusted his messenger bag and caught up with Casey who was walking fast around the top of the quad. "Where are we going?"

Casey wasn't sure. He kept going over the word "date" in his head since the other day, and while he wasn't sure he could just all of a sudden take Daniel to a movie and dinner in the middle of the day, he thought maybe a walk around campus would be a good start.

"The sun's out, so why don't we just go for a walk? We can cut through the practice fields and check out the community park on the other side."

Daniel held tight to the strap of his messenger bag, something Casey noticed him doing when he was nervous or unsure. As they passed between the buildings and along the path through the practice fields, neither of them spoke, and Casey worried that he didn't have anything specific to talk about. Thankfully, Daniel saved the day by complaining.

"The professor wanted to tell me about an internship next spring."

"Really?" Casey said. "That's kinda awesome, isn't it?"

Daniel deflated and hung his head. "I guess. But it would've been nicer if he had asked me about it instead of demanding that I sign up for it."

Casey didn't understand. "What do you mean?"

"He basically told me I had to work with Dr. Yang because I've been slacking on my practical work." His voice trailed off at the end of the sentence. Casey wasn't sure he heard him correctly.

"Practical work? You mean like your sketches? You're painting?"

Daniel looked confused. "I don't really paint anymore," he said. "But sketching, definitely, and other things, I guess. I work a little with sculpture, but I don't seem to have a knack for it."

They walked a little ways more, coming to the last practice field, this one laid out for soccer and reached the edge of the campus property. There was a low wooden fence that marked the border and a small iron gate to allow people to pass through. Casey took the opportunity to run and leap over the fence onto the other side. He turned around to see if Daniel was watching, but he seemed troubled by his conversation, and, head down, he made his way to the gate.

Casey tried to change his mood. "Isn't an internship a good thing? Dr. Yang is head of the department, right?"

Daniel stopped on the other side of the fence as he thought about his answer. They were just on the outside of a play area, the indentation filled with safety mulch. An old-fashioned jungle gym sprouted out of the center. It was late morning on a school day, and the park was deserted. Without answering, Daniel walked over to a set of plastic stairs that led to an upper level. He dropped his messenger bag in the safety mulch and sat on the first step.

"It's a great opportunity, but I would have to be in Philadelphia for the entire semester."

Casey moved over to the jungle gym, grabbed some of the lower bars, and pretended to do pull-ups with his feet firmly on the ground. "Philadelphia's only an hour away. That's not so bad, is it?"

Daniel folded his hands in front of himself and stared at them. Casey wasn't sure if he was thinking of an answer to the question or an answer for Casey. It frustrated him to think that Daniel might tell him something other than how he really felt. He wanted Daniel to trust him. He wanted Daniel to rely on him.

"How do you really feel?" Casey decided not to put the qualifier on the end. How do you really feel about what? He wanted to know how Daniel felt about everything. About the internship. About school. About his father. More importantly, how did Daniel feel about Casey?

"To be honest, I don't know how I feel about anything," Daniel said. He leaned back with a heavy sigh and stared at the clouds. "I feel like everything's moving around me."

Casey walked over and looked down at Daniel, his face as close as he dared. "That's just because you're not moving," Casey said. He jumped backward and climbed on the jungle gym, twisting in and out of the spaces between the metal bar. He climbed easily to the top, since it wasn't much taller than him. He sat down at the highest peak and beat his chest. Conqueror of the mountain.

Daniel laughed and Casey swelled with pride. He waited.

Daniel caught his breath and said, "Monkey bars. That suits you. Figures for a lacrosse player who's always moving around."

Casey slid forward off the dome of bars and landed easily in the safety mulch. "I didn't always play lacrosse. My dad suggested I do that when I came to Woodlawn. Though it was more of an insistence than a suggestion." He moved over to stand under the deck that connected the monkey bars to the stairs where Daniel sat. He grabbed the edge of the deck and swung his feet over the ground, letting his arms and shoulder stretch. "I ran track all through high school. Did hurdles, and I loved it."

He heard Daniel say, "Hurdles huh? That explains a lot."

Casey let go and turned around. Daniel was twisted at a strange angle, making sure he was facing away from Casey. He saw his ears turn red at the tips and, for a second, was wondering what made him so embarrassed. He thought about his comment about the hurdles. Maybe Daniel had noticed him before. Maybe even before he'd noticed Daniel.

He waited to see if Daniel would change the subject, but his ears just got redder, and, still twisted away from Casey, he stood. It looked like he was about to reach for his bag, and Casey thought, if he didn't stop him, he'd lose him.

Casey took three quick steps forward and put his arm around Daniel's shoulder casually, enough that it could be played off as friendly but also with just enough strength to let Daniel know he was serious.

Daniel didn't pull away but slowly turned his face toward Casey. He was only a couple inches shorter than he was, but Casey still had to lean his head down to whisper.

"Come with me."

Gently, he pulled Daniel with him into the space underneath the upper deck of the play set. It was slightly darker here and smelled like moss and late fall leaves. Doing his best not to frighten Daniel, Casey put his own back against the support beam and pulled Daniel close to him. He leaned forward slowly, eyes on Daniel's, waiting to see any resistance in his face. He saw none and kissed him lightly but intentionally.

His own neck and face seemed to burn, and he forced himself to pull away. Daniel's own face had reddened, but he turned his head up, looking directly at Casey. He had never seen eyes this blue and felt like he wanted to know everything that was going on behind them. His body started to tremble as he realized he hadn't taken a breath.

"Is this OK?"

Daniel continued to look directly at him, directly into him, and then nodded. Casey leaned in quickly as if released from a restraint and kissed him deeply, opening Daniel's mouth with his own. He pulled him closer, wrapping his arms around his shoulders and upper body, almost trying to pull him into himself and hold him in place. Daniel's hands moved up his back, fingers trembling. Casey tried to not think about where they were but knew they couldn't stay hidden for long. They would have to stop, but Casey couldn't. Just one moment more.

"Uh," Daniel said, pulling back quickly. "I have to go. I'm gonna be late for class." He didn't let go of Casey right away but stood there, looking at his eyes, then his mouth, and then down at his chest. Daniel's breath came fast, and it took all of Casey's will to loosen his hold. Words failed him. His head was full of wanting to kiss him again.

Daniel backed away and stumbled through the safety mulch. He grabbed his bag and slung it over his shoulder, then ran for the fence. "I'm sorry," he called back. "I'm gonna be late for class."

Daniel disappeared across the fields, running and stumbling, as Casey stood alone, a grown man lovesick under a play set. He put a hand up to his mouth trying to hold on to the memory of Daniel's lips.

22

DANIEL DID NOT HAVE CLASS. In fact, he wasn't sure he was ever going to be able to go to any class ever again. His head was full of fog and flowers for some reason, and his skin seemed to want to break out into goosebumps upon goosebumps. If he stumbled one more time, cutting across the practice field, Daniel seriously thought he would shatter into pieces.

He knew exactly what happened, he wasn't confused, but while he was overwhelmed, a small, dark part of his brain was telling him it was all a joke. But that kiss was no joke. That kiss was serious. And he had to admit to himself that Casey was serious. Serious about him.

How the hell did that happen?

Daniel essentially sleepwalked through the rest of the day. He took care to not leave his apartment, trying to stay clear of campus or any area he was likely to run into Casey. He kept to his room, his head either in his pillow or in his sketchbook. He told himself that he needed to think. He needed to sort out his feelings. In reality, he didn't have any feelings that needed sorting out. He felt excitement, attraction, maybe infatuation, and something he wasn't ready to name. Every time he closed his eyes, he could see an outline from his sketchbook, the one that always seemed to form into Casey.

When did the drawing start? It certainly started before he met the guy, but why? He knew why he was attracted to Casey. He was the opposite of him in so many ways but not in the things that matter. He had a work ethic and a streak of kindness that was rare among men his age, at least in Daniel's experience. He couldn't recall the moment he first noticed him. It's as if one moment Casey all of a sudden became part of the world around him, as if he abruptly came into focus. And now, everywhere he looked, something reminded him of Casey.

When he got back to the apartment, he couldn't look Jess in the eye. He grunted a few answers trying not to show his anxiety. Jess pushed him a little, suspecting that something was wrong. Daniel could sense that Jess was annoyed, and if he explained why he was feeling distant and distracted, there's no way he wasn't going to be upset. He wouldn't call it jealousy, certainly not, but Jess was overprotective in the way that you appreciate when you're young and vulnerable but tends to be stifling as you get older. Daniel avoided confrontations, especially those with stronger personalities than himself. By all accounts, Daniel appeared meek and reserved. But his sense of self was very much intact, and he liked to make space for other people. Add to that a soft-spoken nature and people often thought of him as weak. He would have guessed that was Casey's impression when they first met, but in many small ways, Casey proved him wrong. The man's sincerity reminded Daniel of his father.

Daniel stopped sketching and leaned back from his desk. The comparison between Casey and his father gave him pause. Is the struggle in his relationship with his father part of the reason he was drawn to Casey? Was Casey some sort of replacement? He had to admit they both had this strong nurturing air about them.

But reconnecting with his father over the weekend didn't make him feel more distant to Casey. It brought them closer. Daniel suddenly realized he never properly thanked Casey for his advice.

Half of his mind had been consumed with annoyance over his conversation with Dr. Tate, and the other was preoccupied with the proximity of Casey himself. When Casey put his arm around his shoulders, his whole world contracted to that moment. Was he so lonely that he needed to completely fall into someone else?

Or was it because he was truly falling for Casey?

He leaned forward, putting his elbows on his desk, and ran his hands through his hair, cradling his head as he tried to work it all out. What was he gonna do? If Casey was really interested in him, did he just ruin everything by running away?

He looked at the hastily drawn lines in a sketchbook and closed it in disgust. He didn't have the head for drawing; he didn't have the hand for thinking. He was not in any position to exist as an adult in this world. He turned off the desk lamp, flopped into his bed and tried to sleep. It was 4 o'clock in the afternoon, and Daniel stayed there until morning.

By the time the sun hit Daniel's face the next morning it wasn't the 16 hours of sleep that ran an icy bolt up his spine, but the presence of Casey in the middle of his apartment parking lot, smiling, and waving up at him. For a moment, he wasn't sure what to do and considered bolting back inside and locking the door. He had heard of people in Japan that never left their home and seemed to live quiet, peaceful lives. He wondered if Jess would allow him to change the trajectory of his life and just become a recluse. But his feet started moving, and he was halfway down the steps before he realized he had no idea what to say.

Casey had plenty to say. He stood exactly in his spot, his hands grasping the strap of his duffel bag strap over his shoulder. "I'm very sorry for yesterday. I upset you. It won't happen –"

Daniel raised his hands and shook his head. "It's fine. It's OK."

Casey's face was full of concern, but his eyes were hopeful. Daniel's instinct was to rush forward and pat him on the head, letting him know he hadn't been bad. He smiled, chuckling a bit at himself at the thought.

"I think I was just surprised, but," Daniel struggled to keep eye contact as he said,"but I would like for it to happen again."

His body trembled once the words left his mouth, but the wide grin that broke on Casey's face made it all worthwhile. The man still didn't take a step forward, but he shuffled side-to-side as if he was holding himself back. Daniel took a moment to enjoy the fact that he had that effect on someone like Casey. He didn't understand why, but for right now, he would enjoy that.

"OK. OK." Casey took a deep breath and stood up a little straighter. "Will you go out with me?"

Daniel, not really used to these kinds of interactions, immediately misinterpreted and said, "Sure, where?" He closed his eyes when he realized his mistake.

But Casey didn't miss a beat. "Everywhere, anywhere, all the time."

Daniel opened his eyes and laughed. How could he feel insecure in the face of such earnestness?

"Yes," he finally answered. An alarm on his phone started beeping. "But I really do have to get to class."

"That's why I'm here," Casey said.

They walked side-by-side out of the parking lot, down to the corner, and headed to campus. Once, Daniel wondered if he should reach out and grab Casey's hand, but Casey's hands were clinging to the strap of his duffel bag for the entire walk.

23

THEY BOTH HAD morning classes on Tuesday, though not the same one. Daniel agreed to meet with Casey in the student union and have lunch in the food court. Normally on Tuesdays, he had lunch with Jess, so he texted him to say he was going to be busy. Jess had read the text, but didn't respond for almost half an hour, and when he did, it was just with a short, "Fine." Daniel wasn't sure if he was in trouble, but he was far too nervous about lunch to worry about his roommate.

The food court was laid out like a bicycle wheel with spokes of tables and chairs moving from a central condiment and cutlery station stretching out to a ring of retail and college-sponsored eateries. Daniel normally avoided the food court because of the crowds and noise. That much activity drove him to distraction. On the rare times he found himself in the student union, he would sit near the tall windows on the outer edge. It was quieter and the seats were more comfortable. Plus, he could easily watch and sketch.

Daniel approached the tables, hoping he didn't look like a lost child looking for his parents. He was saved by the bright red hair of Shane McIntyre, one of Casey's teammates and fellow modernism student. Almost as tall as Riley, he stood out as he stood up, and Daniel realized that the team had secured an entire table. He was relieved when Shane waved, recognizing him from his visit to practice. He took comfort in the fact that immediately after he would be able to go back to his apartment and sit quietly alone with his sketchbook and recharge.

Daniel felt a hand on his back and heard a familiar voice in his ear. "Hello, hello." Casey stood next to him and pushed him gently along towards the table. "I hope you don't mind lunch with my teammates. They're also my friends, and they might be a little loud, but they're good guys, and I want you to know them."

Daniel hung his head as he blushed and was propelled forward into the thick of the food court tables. Shane, the redhead sat back down next to the other teammate that was in their modernism class. The blonde nodded at Daniel and pulled his backpack off the chair next to him so Casey and Daniel could sit down. Casey whispered, "Pizza OK?" and Daniel nodded. He felt out of place without Casey. For him, his discomfort felt so palpable that there was an air around him. Other people would notice. But more players soon arrived at the table, two of them arguing and drawing the attention of everyone.

"You were supposed to remind me about that project," Hiro said. He was sulking next to a taller blonde boy who Daniel remembered as the other freshman on the team. He and Hiro noticed Daniel at the table and smiled. "It's the artist. Hello!" He pointed to his own chest. "Hiro, remember?"

Daniel chuckled. "Yes, I remember."

"You're impossible to forget Hiro," came Shane's voice. "You never shut up."

The other freshman laughed, then sat his backpack down on the seat across from Daniel. He said a quiet, "Hello," to him and left to get something to eat. Hiro dropped his backpack on the floor and followed him.

"Those two are either going to destroy us or lead us to the league championship," said the man next to Daniel. He was eating a chicken and rice bowl while he watched the freshmen walk away.

Daniel's stomach growled. "Destroy the team?" he asked. He watched the freshman push each other as they lined up for barbecue. "Could they do that?"

"Brett's being dramatic. It's a consequence of never opening his mouth," Shane said leaning forward. Brett took another bite of his lunch and looked at Daniel. He shrugged, confirming his friend's assessment.

Riley and another man unfamiliar to Daniel sat down at the far end of the table, engrossed in their own conversation. Even though he'd only seen Riley on a few occasions and talked to him even less, he could tell the man was tired. Something about his face gave Daniel the impression he wanted to be somewhere else. Riley's eyes went from his companion to Daniel. He stared as if trying to understand what he was seeing.

Daniel flashed a crooked smile, and Riley forced one in return. He immediately turned back to the other player. Already feeling insecure, Daniel took the hint that he might not belong here.

"You're in the wrong seat," Casey said from behind him. A tray with two slices of pepperoni pizza appeared on the table next to him.

"This one's yours. You sit on the end here, OK?"

Daniel started to get up, automatically. "Why?"

Casey sat down his own tray, with three slices of what looked like veggie loaded pizza. "You're left-handed, I figured you probably eat left-handed too. This way you won't be bumping into anyone."

Daniel sat down slowly at the edge of the table, his left side free of blockage. He was left-handed and was surprised that Casey had noticed, but when it came to eating, it didn't matter. He was used to accommodating whomever he sat with, so when he got to the table, he didn't think twice about sitting in the seat offered by Brett. He wasn't used to this kind of consideration. He wasn't used to people noticing anything about him. It made him feel important, but it also made him feel a little uneasy. Daniel wasn't sure he liked how automatically he switched his seat.

The new arrangement put Daniel physically on the outside of the group of teammates. Casey wasn't the center of the conversations, that role seemed to be held alternately between Shane and Hiro, the two most talkative of the group. Brett and Kellen mirrored each other in their silence and occasional shrug to their friends. Riley and the other teammate, whom Daniel eventually learned was their captain and senior, seemed to be having a serious discussion of their own, oblivious to the rest of them.

Casey joined each conversation in turn, making comments and laughing. He would turn and ask Daniel for his opinion or ask how his lunch was. The whole time Casey kept his left leg pressed against Daniel's right. He tried to focus on anything but the sense of them touching and every time he felt he'd settled down, Casey would move, applying more pressure or leaning closer, any number of a million little things to remind Daniel that he was right there.

Under the table.

They hadn't held hands across campus, and now, above the table, Casey was physically distant. He hadn't introduced Daniel to any of the teammates. He relied on his friends to introduce themselves. Only Kellen had to be introduced to him by name and that was after they had a bit of a conversation. And Doug was just mentioned when Casey saw Daniel looking his way.

The physical space of the table and the conversational topics of practices and schedules kept Daniel so far on the margins that he may as well have been in another room. And that dark voice in the back of his head popped up and said *well, you don't belong here, right?*

He thought back to that moment yesterday with Casey and that kiss that was so insistent and determined. He had no misunderstanding about how Casey felt at that moment.

At that moment. When they were alone. Hidden.

Daniel lost his appetite. He didn't like where his mind was going, and he wanted to think better of Casey. Everything that Casey had done had made him think better of him, and he felt safe around him. But he wondered if Casey thought it was too early to be open. It was only that morning that Casey asked him out, but would he tell his teammates right away?

Would he ever tell them?

He pushed the tray and spent the rest of the lunch, nursing his iced tea, thinking, listening to the laughter. He wished he was sitting alone by the windows, sketching but never part of the scene.

24

―――

CASEY STOOD under a cluster of walnut trees outside the science building, waiting for Riley to be done with his class. They usually walked home together on these days since both had shifts at their respective part-time jobs, Casey at a convenience store, and Riley at the bar. He often wondered if he should get his bartending certificate because Riley seemed to make good money in tips. But Riley was also tall and quiet, and he suspected that many of those tips were not necessarily because of his drink mixing skills.

He was feeling light and excited, enjoying the memory of sitting with Daniel at lunch with all of his friends. It was if all of his favorite things were in the same space and he could reach out and touch every single one. Maybe "things" was a poor way of phrasing it, but the little kid inside Casey was hopping up and down, uninterested in nuance. He could still feel the ghost of Daniel's leg touching his own.

He found it so hard to hold back, to not put his arms around Daniel's shoulders and hang onto him. To sit and watch his eyes dart about as he watched the people in the food court. He practically had to sit on his hands to stop poking Daniel's little cheeks that seemed to puff up every time he took a bite of pizza. It was their first meal together, and it was all he could do to not react with laughter and kisses.

Unfortunately, it was the part of the week where their schedules were the busiest and didn't match up at all until their class the next morning. It frustrated Casey, not being with him all the time, but he was trying to take things slow. He didn't want to scare Daniel away by coming on too strong, and he wasn't sure how comfortable Daniel would be as part of a public couple. They hadn't had a chance to talk about important things outside of that one conversation in the library. There were still so many things about Daniel he didn't know yet, and he wanted to tread carefully. Hurting him was the last thing he wanted to do.

When his phone rang, he fumbled getting it out of his pocket, too excited to talk to Daniel again. His face fell when he saw "Dad" on the screen. Since there was no one around, Casey sighed and answered the call.

"Hey Dad. What's up?"

His father's voice, a slightly deeper version of his own, was clipped, his breath heavy, as if he was walking fast. His voice echoed as if he were moving through the staff hallways of the hotel. Probably from one meeting to the next.

"What's this I hear about you changing majors?"

Casey took a deep breath and listened to his father's heavy footsteps. He sarcastically felt thankful the man could pencil him in between meetings. "I want to explore some options. That's all."

"The business major is gonna give you the most options, son. I thought we talked about this."

"You talked about it. But it's my decision." Casey thought he would add more, but he wasn't exactly sure how to explain. He'd struggled during his two years as a business major, not because the content was difficult, but because he was disinterested in the machinations of the business world. This was his father's world, and while he didn't resent his father, he felt that there was something more out there for him.

"What decision have you made about your future? What options do you think you have to explore?"

It was a fair question, Casey thought, and certainly something he had turned over in his head. But recently, he had been so concerned with his relationship with Daniel that his change in major at the beginning of the semester seemed like forever ago. When he made the decision, he felt a weight lift off his shoulders. He never had any intention of following in his father's footsteps into the hotel business, but he had been so completely convinced that a business degree was the baseline for any kind of success he never tried anything else. It wasn't until he started taking the supplementary art classes over the summer that he thought there was much more to the world.

In a way, falling for Daniel had opened up so many possibilities for him. He sat there holding the phone to his face, looking out over the quad. Students began emptying out of the classroom buildings. All of a sudden, he had so much to thank Daniel for, and he desperately wanted to see him right away to do so.

"Come home this weekend so we can talk properly." His father didn't ask. His father rarely asked for anything.

"I don't think so," Casey answered. "I've got tests and a project to work on, so I think I'll stay here this weekend"

"What? I didn't hear you," his father's voice had grown faint, and Casey suspected he had walked all the way into the lower levels of the hotel, where cell phone signals had trouble getting past the thick walls and the HVAC machinery.

Casey was about to repeat himself when his father interrupted. "You will come home whether you confirm with me or not. We will discuss this with your mother. And I will make you see reality."

"Wait a minute," Casey said, but his father had already ended the call.

The lightness he had been feeling since lunchtime left, and his whole body felt heavy and tired. As he got older, it was harder to reason with his father. Especially as Casey got bigger and kinder in a lot of ways. He seemed to be far more influenced by his mother's personality than his father's, much to his father's consternation. It wasn't an abusive relationship by any means, it was just that two people that loved each other very much had very different ideas of what the future held.

Casey was starting to resent that no one thought to consult with him about his own life. For the first time that he could remember, he wanted to be the architect of that future. For the first time in his whole life, if he was being honest, he felt like he had someone to build a future with.

The flow of students increased, and Riley appeared at his side. He looked as weary as Casey suddenly felt. "You ready to go?"

Riley only shrugged. They took their usual route home in silence. There had been tension between them since Casey told Riley about his feelings for Daniel. He still wasn't completely sure why Riley didn't seem immediately happy for him. It's not that it wasn't obvious to Riley, Casey thought, but still you want to support your best friend, right? By the time they got to the parking lot of their apartment building, Casey's annoyance that started with his father's phone call had grown with the silence of his best friend.

"Something bothering you?" Casey said it with genuine interest, but couldn't stop the sharpness of his tone.

Riley continued walking a few steps and stopped. He stood

still for a moment before turning around, and Casey realized Riley's typical reserved demeanor had broken. "What do you mean?" His voice was forceful. It wasn't a question; it was an accusation.

"Things have been weird between us, and you didn't say anything about lunch today?" He assumed Riley was going to ask him about Daniel, about their relationship and how things were going. It was one of the things he was preparing to talk about on their walk home.

"Is it my business?"

Casey couldn't read Riley's expression. "You're my best friend. Of course it's your business"

Riley tilted his head to the side. "You two dating now?"

Casey couldn't stop the smile forming on his face and the sense of pride he felt in his chest. "Yup"

"Couldn't tell." Riley said flatly. "Well, *I* could, but are you gonna tell the rest of the team?"

Casey furrowed his brows trying to see where this conversation was going. "Eventually. I don't wanna make Daniel uncomfortable by saying too much, I guess." Saying it out loud made the excuse seem weak.

Riley clicked his tongue. "Bullshit! You're just gonna half-ass this relationship, aren't you?"

Casey opened his mouth but had no words to fill it. Riley had never snapped at him like this. His tone was impatient and annoyed, but then the meaning of his best friend's words hit him in the gut. "What do you mean half-ass?"

"You keep things quiet. Why? With everything that you did to get here and now you wanna hide?"

Casey just stood there, torn between arguing with Riley and thinking that maybe he was right. He trusted Riley's instinct and his advice. He was always the first person he would talk to about damn near anything. He was split into two, and with each half of him going in a different direction, Casey ended up paralyzed and lost for words.

"Whatever," Riley said and started walking in the opposite direction. As he passed Casey, he paused, "You do what you want, but it's not just your life right now, is it?"

25

Daniel sat behind Casey in their modernism class and worried. He'd never seen Casey so lackluster and tired. He normally jogged up the stairs to reach his seat, but today, he seemed weighed down. Casey barely glanced at Daniel when he said "Hello."

Before the professor started his lecture, Casey spun around. "I'm sorry. I had to work late last night, and I'm beat."

Daniel smiled and almost reached out his hand. "No problem. Is there anything I can do?"

Casey smiled with genuine warmth and shook his head. "I'm gonna head back and take a nap after class. Will you come to practice today?" He'd lowered his head to not be overheard but looked up at Daniel. It gave him the appearance of a little boy in trouble.

That look was unfair, Daniel thought. He was the one in trouble. He pretended to look at his phone calendar, checking to see if he had any conflicts. He knew his schedule was clear but needed a second to think. He was still processing his feelings from the day before, feelings of being kept on the outside and almost hidden. He hoped he was overthinking things, in fact he was most definitely overthinking things, but his emotions had been in a tail-spin all year, and Daniel had no confidence when it came to his heart.

Daniel decided that he could figure it out by trying again. How will Casey treat him around the whole team, not just his closest friends? He didn't like putting himself in a position to get hurt, but he had to admit, he'd put himself in that position the moment he talked to Casey on the first day.

"Sure," he finally said. "I don't have anything this afternoon."

Casey's face lit up. "Great," he said with exhausted enthusiasm.

"Mr. Stanfield. Have I moved the screen?"

Casey rolled his eyes and turned back around to the front of the class. Professor Tate, satisfied, began his lecture. Daniel only half listened and instead sketched butterflies in the margins of his notes.

His phone rang as he was just entering the student union, a typical shortcut to get to the practice fields without having to walk around the massive building. When he saw the call from his father, his stomach sank out of habit. He found a quiet spot away from the rest of the students, and he answered the call.

"Hi Dad. What's up?"

"Kiddo," his father said. His voice was far more upbeat than Daniel had heard in a while. The lightness of his tone surprised him. "I just wanted to check in and see how you were doing."

Daniel shrugged even though he was on the phone. "I think I'm doing OK. You sound... good?"

Rich laughed. "I guess compared to the last few months. I won't keep you. I just wanted to run something by you."

Daniel had no idea where this conversation was going. The dread that he had felt before he answered remained, but it was smaller. "OK." He didn't know what else to say.

"I'm thinking of driving down to see your aunt in a week or

two. She just got that new house and has been complaining that there's a lot of little things that need fixing here and there. I thought I'd make myself useful."

Daniel's aunt lived in Maryland, and while it was a short drive from their house, he wasn't sure his father was ready to do a trip like that by himself. It's not that he didn't trust him, it's just that this positive change in him might flip at any moment. He worried that his father being two hundred miles away, and with Daniel without a car, he wouldn't be able to help him.

"I didn't know she bought a house?" It didn't matter if she bought a house or a horse, Daniel wanted to keep his dad on the phone for a minute or two. He had to think if it was alright for him to feel hesitant about his dad doing something for himself. It felt like the man was asking for his permission, and while Daniel understood their roles had reversed since his mother died, he expected that emotional caregiving to last much longer.

Then again, his father was just going to see his sister, and maybe spending time with family other than Daniel was a good idea. Surely, he saw his wife every time he looked at Daniel's face. Daniel couldn't imagine how painful that must be.

"I think it's a great idea. Do you know when you're going?"

Richard's voice sounded relieved. "No, not yet. I have to figure out my work schedule and see if it lines up with hers. But I'll let you know."

Daniel saw a familiar face heading his way and nodded in recognition to Hiro as he approached. He pointed to his phone, so the freshman knew he was still on a call. Hiro stopped, gave him the thumbs up, and waited. Daniel wasn't sure what the freshman could possibly want with him.

"I'm not gonna keep you any longer," Rich said. "You have a good day and give me a call over the weekend, OK?"

Daniel nodded, then said, "Sure have a good day."

"Love you!" Rich said.

Daniel looked away from Hiro who waited patiently. "Love you too," and hung up.

He took a moment to see if any other messages came through while he was on the call, and not surprisingly, none had appeared. He slipped the phone back into his pocket and turned to his new pal. "Hi."

"Hey there," Hiro said. "I saw you as I was cutting through." He pointed to the large door that opened upon the group of practice fields behind the student union. "What are you up to?"

Daniel had no idea why the freshman wanted to chat with him. Casey had mentioned that he'd tried to get into his good graces for his mother's business, but they'd already worked that out, Daniel thought. He thought maybe Hiro wanted to stay in Casey's orbit, which now apparently contained himself.

"I was just heading to practice, too," Daniel said. He held up his hands when Hiro gave him a searching look. "No, no. Not *to* practice." He wasn't sure if he should say he was meeting Casey, but he didn't want to lie to the kid. Hiro's face was open and honest, and Daniel had the distinct feeling he was handling something delicate when he talked with him.

"I thought I'd do some more sketching today, since the weather is better."

Hiro pouted. "Aw. I thought you'd realized how awesome lacrosse was and you decided to play."

Daniel laughed. "There is no way I'd be able to do what you do," he said. The idea of him running around like Casey, or even Hiro, amused him. "I think a pencil is the safest stick for me."

Hiro stared at him. "Heh."

Daniel didn't understand what Hiro meant. He was about to change the subject when Hiro took a little jump away from Daniel. "Let's go!"

His body moved on his own. Daniel noticed that he automatically followed someone with that much exuberance. He'd have to keep an eye on that.

Hiro held open the door, and they exited into a soft breeze and a busy patio. Most of the chill had retreated, and students had brought their meals outside. Hiro leapt down the stairs that led to the fields. Daniel took each step, not wanting to fall. He hadn't been back to his apartment to drop off his textbooks, and his messenger bag was pulling him off balance.

"Ah, look," Hiro said. He'd stopped at the edge of the gravel path that ran the circumference of the grassy area. At the far corner stood Casey. Daniel was about to raise his hand to catch his eye when a young woman ran up to him and gave him a hug. It was a quick hug, a friendly hug, and nothing-to-be-misunderstood hug. But it wasn't a first-time hug. It was not a courteous hug. It was the hug that you give to someone that you have hugged before because you know it's OK to hug them. Daniel was overthinking, but he was also watching Casey look handsome and comfortable hugging a beautiful girl with a ponytail.

Hiro came back to Daniel and stood near his shoulder. "Who's that? His girlfriend?"

Daniel turned to Hiro not wanting to keep watching. He didn't know what to say, so he answered honestly, even though it was a surprise to him when it came out of his mouth. "I don't know. Maybe."

Hiro said nothing for a moment and seemed to be thinking. Then he turned to Daniel and muttered, "All right."

Without another word between them, Hiro and Daniel made their way along the gravel path in the opposite direction of Casey. A few seconds later, Daniel heard someone running fast along the gravel path, and before he could turn around, Casey was at his side.

"Hey there," Casey said.

"Hi." Daniel said, while keeping his eyes on the ground before him. It was only after they walked a little farther that he realized Hiro had left them, running off to join the rest of the team on the field.

"The nap really helped," said Casey. "And I'm sorry about earlier."

Daniel didn't know what "earlier" meant. Earlier in class? Earlier at lunch? Earlier when he had his arms around some girl? He flinched at his own thoughts. He hated feeling like this. It made him feel stupid and weak.

"It's fine," Daniel said. "I'm glad you got some rest."

They kept walking, Daniel feeling Casey's eyes on him the entire time. He kept his eyes on the ground before him, hands tight on the strap of his messenger bag to keep it from pulling him off balance. When they were about ten feet from the side line, Daniel stopped.

"This is good." he eased his messenger bag off his shoulder and let it drop with a thud into the grass. "This is as far as I'll go."

Casey watched him and opened his mouth, as if to say something, but then just smiled. He jogged over to the rest of the team.

Daniel pulled his sketchbook and pencil out of his messenger bag. He checked the clouds, hoping it wouldn't rain, but secretly thinking it might.

26

—————

Daniel immersed himself in his work so deeply that when the team gathered at the end of practice he was surprised. A few stray droplets had dotted his current drawing, and it seemed that another practice would be cut short due to rain. He packed up his things and stood awkwardly waiting while the team listened to their captain's instructions. He felt conspicuous.

When the team was released, Hiro was the first to reach Daniel. He couldn't understand how someone could have so much energy after such a rigorous practice. This time the freshman wasn't alone but had brought his teammate with him.

"Did you get some good pictures today?" Hiro asked. "Can I see them?"

"I just put everything away," Daniel said. "Plus, I'm pretty sure this rain is about to get a lot worse."

Hiro and Kellen both looked up in the sky and then back to Daniel. "Well, show us next time you come to practice. I wanna see if you drew me."

Kellen smacked Hiro on the shoulder. "Leave him alone."

He turned to him. "What? You're just jealous cause nobody wants to draw you."

"What are you guys doing?" Casey said as he approached. The freshman seemed to almost stand at attention with Casey in their midst. Daniel thought that was a credit to Casey's talent, or perhaps his personality. He seemed to have a way of attracting people toward him.

"I just wanted to see what he was drawing," Hiro said.

"Not today," Casey replied and put his hand on Daniel's shoulder. "We're gonna go eat."

"Oh, let us come with—"

Casey poked the top of his lacrosse stick into Hiro's chest, gently holding him back. "No. Back." He nodded to the other freshman. "Kellen, take him back to the dorms."

Kellen nodded and grabbed the back of Hiro's sweatshirt, dragging him away.

"He's quite attached to you," Daniel said as they left the field.

Casey shrugged. "He's a good kid, but I'm still not sure about his intentions. Best to keep him at arm's length. Or stick, I guess." He flipped his stick in the air, caught it, and rested it on his shoulder.

"Where do you want to eat?" Daniel asked, just as the rain started.

"Run," Casey yelled and cut across the path to the main road. Daniel barely kept up.

The size of Casey and Riley's apartment shocked him. He and Jess had a normal, two-bedroom apartment a few blocks away. It wasn't big by any standards, but the two of them had their own space and privacy. Casey and Riley shared a studio apartment with a basic kitchenette and bathroom. They'd put a thick bookcase between the two twin beds that dominated the main area of the apartment. Each roommate had a small desk crammed between his bed and the wall. And, much to Daniel's surprise, both men were neat and tidy.

"We wanted to stay as close to campus as possible for as little money as possible," Casey explained. He took Daniel's messenger bag and hung it on a coat stand near the door. "Close to campus so we can sleep later, and cheap because we're both paying our way through Woodlawn."

Daniel didn't know where to go, but just a step or two and he'd be across the room. He tried to stand casually near the door, not wanting to have to choose where to sit. He could take a seat at one of the desks, or sit on one of the beds. His head was getting cloudy. As neat as the place was, the whole room smelled like Casey.

"Hold on," Daniel said abruptly. "I thought you were here on scholarship or legacy?"

Casey laughed. "Legacy is just about admissions, and the only way to avoid that would be to go somewhere else." He opened the small refrigerator and took out a sports drink. He offered one to Daniel, who declined. "I didn't have a scholarship until sophomore year. I walked on to the lacrosse team as a freshman."

Daniel still felt conscious of just standing by the door. "Is that why you have so many part time jobs?"

Casey sat at the foot of his bed and patted the mattress next to him. Daniel's feet moved before he was even aware of walking.

"I have two and a third with the catering company on occasion. That's Riley's gig, and I just help out when they need extra hands."

Daniel sat down, only partially taking in the conversation. The soft creak from the mattress as he sat down seemed to echo in the room. He tried to position himself in the perfect spot, not too far to fall off the edge and not too close to do, what? All of a sudden, Daniel needed to choose what he did and didn't want to do, right here and now.

He considered just throwing himself off the bed for good measure. Instead, he said something provocative.

"Don't you and Riley need more privacy? What do you do when—" he trailed off finally understanding the implications. The question had started as more curiosity than anything. But he'd always had a hard time interpreting romantic situations. Lack of experience was probably the issue. Daniel suddenly felt completely out of his depth.

"It's not really been an issue," Casey said matter-of-factly. "I mean, neither of us are here all that often. Between work, school, and practice, we mostly just eat and sleep here."

Daniel looked around the room, crammed with books and clothes but still organized. He could see why it would be hard to bring anyone here. He imagined girls wouldn't be too impressed.

"Besides, I've not really known Riley to be dating anyone, to be honest." Casey scratched his chin. "I guess I just assumed he wasn't into that, like he was ace or something." He stretched and leaned back, his elbows on the mattress.

"Did he tell you that?" Daniel asked, genuinely curious.

Casey turned to him and tilted his head. "Not in so many words."

"How many words?" Daniel asked.

A small smile played at the corner of Casey's mouth. "None?"

He leaned forward and put his hand on Daniel's cheek, pulling his face toward his own. Daniel let himself be led forward and closed his eyes as their lips touched. He'd been remembering their first kiss in the playground since it happened. It had surprised him, but this one surpassed that one. It was expected, even wanted, and Daniel felt an urgency replace his earlier fear.

He twisted himself around so he could wrap his arms around Casey's waist and pulled himself into him. He was only slightly smaller than Casey, but Casey was all muscle which made him harder to budge, so Daniel decided to just place himself where *he* wanted to be.

Casey suddenly pulled back and stood up. "Gah," he said as he pulled off his shirt. "It smells." He flopped back down on the bed and grabbed Daniel, this time around his waist. "I may smell too," Casey whispered. Daniel inhaled deeply, drinking him in. He ran his hands over Casey's shoulders, up the back of his neck and into his hair. It was as soft as Daniel suspected. He'd wondered every time he drew those soft curls how they'd feel under his fingers. Had he really wondered then? Back then? Who cares, he thought and allowed himself to be pulled forward.

Then, the world exploded.

"Whoa. What the hell, Casey?"

Daniel rolled over and sat up. Casey's future-self stood at the door. An older man with the same eyes, same hair, same build filled the doorway, a look of surprise on his face. Daniel's heart raced and his thoughts scrambled, trying to understand the situation and wasn't sure what to do. He turned toward Casey, who only lay back on the bed. His elbow's propping him up with a look of annoyance on his face.

Daniel took a deep breath and saw Riley appear behind the man. Casey's friend shook his head and then turned around and walked out. No one was saying anything, and Daniel felt the sound of his heartbeat filling the room.

He got a glimpse of his messenger bag hanging by the door and that gave him all the direction he needed. He leapt off the bed, lunged toward the messenger bag, grabbed it, knocked over the hat stand, and ran out the door. He thought he would hear yelling behind him, but all was quiet. He reached the stairs and heard nothing but the echoes of his footsteps. By the time he got into the parking lot, he was starting to get a stitch in his side. Daniel hadn't had this much physical activity in a long time. He wasn't sure his body could take it.

Holy shit, Daniel thought. Is that what Casey's going to look like?

He shook his head, wondering why that was the first thing he thought of. As he stood in the parking lot, he quickly realized no one was coming. No one was running down the stairs to see if he was alright. No one was calling to ask him to come back. No one was there at all.

He caught sight of someone nearby and saw Riley disappearing down a side street. Daniel didn't think he could deal with this insecurity any longer, and if this relationship was actually going to be a thing, he needed some answers. He had a feeling a source of some might be heading toward campus right now.

27

———————

By the time he realized Daniel was gone, it was too late. He sat forward on the edge of his bed and stared at the floor. He was torn between his anger at his father and his worry over Daniel. Everybody seemed to be pulling him in different directions, and over the last couple of weeks, he seemed to have lost his ability to express his feelings. Especially between his father and Riley, the pressure of disapproval bared down on him.

All he'd wanted was to spend some time with Daniel and find out why things had gotten weird and distant. Casey thought Daniel was getting more comfortable with him, and he certainly seemed comfortable kissing him. They were at the very beginning of their relationship, and it was already slipping away.

"Aren't you going after him?" His father leaned against the door jamb, leaving space in the doorway.

"What?"

"You should go after him," he repeated, "unless he's just for fun."

Casey fumed at the comment and was about to set the man straight when a T-shirt flew into his face.

"At least put a shirt on."

Casey did as he was told and stayed on the bed. Too many emotions were vying for dominance inside him, and with the last few days of work, school, practice, Daniel had sapped him of so much energy he was even losing the will to fight with his father. "Why are you here?"

"You hung up on me," the man said.

Casey screwed up his face. "No, I didn't. You did."

His father held his gaze for a while, as if he was trying to read his son's thoughts. Eventually, he shrugged. "Whatever. I also had a meeting with someone here, and I thought I would check up on you." He slowly inspected the tiny apartment, taking in all their belongings crammed into the space.

He settled his gaze back on Casey. "I see you're enjoying your time."

Casey sighed. The conversation wasn't going anywhere, as usual, and every moment he spent listening to his father's quips, Daniel got farther away. He stood up, grabbed his phone, and tried to leave the apartment. His father put a hand on his chest, stopping him.

"You come home this weekend." It wasn't a request.

"No. I have—"

"Come home, and I'll leave you alone the rest of the year."

Casey searched the man's face for a trick, but his father was just as honest and open as himself. They were peas in a pod, his grandmother used to say. That had been alright by Casey when he was little, when his father had been his hero. These days it was a burden.

"I have work," Casey tried, knowing it wouldn't matter.

"Call off and come home." His father walked out of the apartment and stood on the front stoop. "I won't order you. It won't work." He paused. "Your mother wants you home."

Casey sighed and gave in. "Fine," he said.

His father looked at him for a moment as if he had more to say. Casey raised his eyebrows, waiting, but the man just gave a small smile and shrugged. He waved as he walked away.

Casey went inside and checked his work schedule, making a mental list of who to call. But first, he tried to get Daniel on the phone, but there was no answer. He fell back onto the bed and stared at the ceiling. How was he going to explain what just happened to Daniel? Did he even know? His father just showed up while they were kissing and Daniel took off.

And Casey didn't immediately go after him. That's the part that even Casey didn't understand. Why didn't he chase him? Was it just his father or something else?

For a moment, Casey thought that the distance between him and Daniel might be his fault. He wondered if he'd read the whole situation wrong and Daniel misunderstood. He tried calling him again, and again the call went to voice mail. He didn't leave a message. He had no idea what to say.

As the anger and confusion left his body, exhaustion took over, and within a minute, Casey was sound asleep.

28

AFTER CATCHING HIS BREATH, Daniel took off running again in the hopes of catching up with Riley. He was surprised how fast he reached him, until he realized Riley had stopped to wait for him. Daniel slowed and then stopped, bending over again to catch his breath and deal with a stitch in his side.

"I heard you coming, so I thought I'd wait," Riley said.

Daniel was surprised. "How did you know it was me?"

"I can tell by the pace of the footsteps. You're slow."

His breathing slowed, and Daniel watched Riley's face closely to see if his comment was meant as a joke. Riley's face was stonier than normal, and it made him nearly impossible to read.

Riley nodded in the direction of the apartment building. "Are they still arguing back there?"

Daniel shrugged. "I'm not sure." He wanted to add something more. Maybe ask one of the thousand questions going on in his brain, but he never had a full conversation with Riley and didn't completely know how to approach him. He'd run after him to get answers, and here he was, unable to ask questions. Thankfully, Riley solved the problem himself.

"It's probably not because of you, if that's what you're worried about."

The honesty of his remark took Daniel off balance. Immediately, he wondered if he was being self-centered and thinking that everything in the world, particularly the bad parts, were centered around him. He's always understood himself to be insecure, but every once in a while, he had to be reminded that with insecurity comes a healthy dose of self-importance. In reality, very little hinges on what Daniel Marsden does or does not do.

Daniel felt he needed to apologize to someone. "Well, I'm sorry to you too."

Riley raised his eyebrows, a sudden break in his stony demeanor. "Nothing for you to be sorry about."

Daniel appreciated Riley's comment, but he didn't think he'd be satisfied until he discovered where he was specifically at fault. "But you seem annoyed—"

Riley let out an exasperated sigh. His shoulders drooped, and his head lulled to the side as he looked into the distance beyond Daniel and probably beyond the immediate world. He seemed to deflate, and Daniel had the impression that Riley held the world on his shoulders.

"My life has, uhm, gotten pretty annoying lately."

Instinctively, Daniel said, "Ah, sorry."

Riley shot him a slightly angry look. "Again, not about you. Not really."

The qualifier echoed in Daniel's head, but he thought the third apology waiting on his tongue would only burden Riley further.

"Did he ask you out, like officially?"

Embarrassed by the question, Daniel felt his face grow warm as he looked down at the sidewalk. "Yes."

"But he didn't tell anyone, did he?" Riley's voice was soft.

Daniel would've expected a line like that to come from a place less kind.

He didn't know how to answer. He wasn't even sure if he should shake his head.

"Well, he told me, but I had already figured it out."

Riley paused, and in the silence, Daniel mustered the courage to look up. Riley's face had softened into one of concern.

"He's not hiding you." It was a statement made confidently. "He's scared. He's scared that you'll be scared, or some nonsense." Riley shook his head.

"He's an idiot," Riley continued, his exasperation overtaking his concern. "You're gonna have to account for that."

Daniel chuckled, and while it wouldn't have been the way he described Casey, not at all, he thought it endearing that his best friend seemed to think of him that way. He had hoped to get to know Casey at least as well as Riley, but the more doubt that rose in his mind, the less likely that felt.

Riley continued, though he seemed to be tired of the conversation. "He's a people pleaser, that's why he's in this mess with his father. He won't do what *he* wants. He always does what the people around him want." He looked around the empty streets.

"Honestly, I don't know what to tell you." He appeared to be looking a long way off, and Daniel had the impression that Riley was finished with *this* conversation and already thinking about his next somewhere else. "I'm not one to give relationship advice."

Daniel nodded, not really sure what to say as his negative thoughts kept getting in the way of replying. While every bit of his being wanted to apologize one more time, he focused on the phrase "people pleaser" and found that his brain could easily weave that into the insecurity he felt the moment Casey showed interest.

Maybe Casey was only responding to Daniel's own attraction. Maybe, for some reason, he wanted to be friends with Daniel but saw that maybe Daniel wanted something more. Had he indicated, in some way, his attraction to Casey? He thought he hid it rather well, considering he'd had so much practice hiding his feelings. But maybe Casey, idiot that Riley thought he was, was attuned to what people want. It made sense to Daniel that someone labeled a "people pleaser" would probably be very aware of Daniel's feelings.

Riley interrupted his ruminations. "I have to get going. Are you OK?"

Daniel kept his eyes focused somewhere on the sidewalk below, but nodded and said, "Yeah, thanks for stopping and answering my questions."

Riley took a few steps in the direction of campus. "You know, you didn't really ask any questions. All you did was apologize." He paused, looking closely at Daniel. "You may be just as much of an idiot as he is."

Riley walked away, leaving Daniel alone on the sidewalk. His thoughts bounced back and forth between kissing Casey and that silence as he'd run from the apartment.

Daniel turned his face to the sky, trying to keep the tears from running down his face. The clouds that plagued them all afternoon had cleared, leaving the night sky full of stars and a new clarity upon himself.

29

DANIEL WAS RELIEVED that the practical art room was nearly empty. A few students worked at project tables in the far corner of the long, narrow room. They appeared to be constructing prototypes of buildings, so Daniel assumed they were architecture students. From the far end of the work room, he watched the students carefully stack intricate cardboard models on a mounting board, creating a light brown cityscape. They seemed comfortable together and cheered each other's efforts.

He sat at a small table near the lockers, far from the door but still a good source of daylight. He decided to spend the day going through some of his old sketchbooks and working on his sculpture homework as a way to get caught up but also distract himself. He wasn't answering any of Casey's phone calls, and the last text message had been over an hour ago. He didn't think Casey was the type to give up, but he was probably the type to understand when it was time to wait. Daniel still didn't know what he was going to say when he talked to him.

Art majors had their own lockers at this end of the room. Daniel unlocked his and pulled out a sketchbook at random.

When he saw the date scrawled at the top, he realized it was his sketch book from the beginning of spring, earlier than the one he carried now. These are the sketches he did when his mother was still alive, when life was so much more normal than it was now. He looked down at the pages and saw a lot of people walking in the park near his home, kids playing baseball at a field near his old high school. He could tell when the studies turned to campus life as all of the subjects became young adults with backpacks and heavy winter coats. He used to enjoy sitting in the café on the edge of the quad, sketching people during class change.

He could see the evolution of his illustrations. His lines were simpler in some cases. The face was more of an impression than details. Daniel always wondered why he wasn't interested so much in re-creating faces but always focused on movement and position of the body as a whole. Perhaps faces were too personal. He flipped over to another page of a faceless group of students. Perhaps he needed to see them as subjects instead of people.

Sometimes we avoid looking at the things we don't want others to see, he thought.

The next page made him stop. It was an obvious sketch of Casey, and he was surprised to see one this far back in time. He knew that towards the end of the semester, he had noticed Casey and started sketching him in his other book but to find one here surprised him. He didn't remember this image specifically. Normally, he could picture himself working on the piece but not this time. He couldn't get a sense of the light, of where he was on campus, of the sounds, nothing about the moment he sketched this but a feeling of warmth. He didn't completely understand that. Maybe the day had been unseasonably warm, and he'd decided to sit outside.

It was also unusual because Casey wasn't in the midst of some athletic movement, whether running across campus or leaping over a fence. He seemed to be sitting, maybe on the wall outside the science building or on a bench near the president's house, but just sitting, arms folded, legs stretched out before him. One of the few students not looking at his phone. Daniel wracked his brain trying to remember this moment and just couldn't. But it was obvious that he'd been drawn toward Casey for a while.

If anything, that only strengthened his doubt about Casey's feelings. If Casey was only responding to Daniel, then here's proof that Daniel had stronger feelings than he wanted to admit, or at least for a longer time. He quickly flipped past the sketch and found more of what he'd done before: Casey running. Casey walking with other students. On a page of physical studies, with hands and feet and chins and ears was a pair of shoulders that could only be Casey's.

A loud cry from the students at the far end of the room, and Daniel looked up in time to see one of the cardboard skyscrapers leaning precariously over the table. The group scrambled to right it again. Even in a crisis, they seemed to be having fun. It must be the same for the team, he thought. He couldn't help but place himself on the outside of such a close-knit group. Daniel envied that. He flipped again in the sketchbook and came across a familiar pose. This had to have been one of the early studies for his painting that he...

"Mr. Marsden."

Professor Tate stood in the middle of the practical room with three canvases under his arm. He dropped them off in one of the display racks usually reserved for student work. After unloading his burden, the professor approached Daniel's table, not with purpose, but curiosity. "You're working?"

"Not really. I'm just going through some old sketchbooks." Daniel wanted to lean forward to cover up his sketches but thought that would look suspicious.

"Hiding?"

Daniel looked up to see the professor looking straight at him, a slight smirk on his face. "What?"

"You look like you're about to melt into the corner back here."

Daniel instinctively turned to look at the corner and then back at Dr. Tate. The man seemed to realize he had made Daniel uncomfortable. He looked away, put his hand on the back of his neck, and miscalculated his attempt to change the subject. "How's your project coming along? Casey doing his part?"

Daniel swallowed. Casey was doing more than his part considering he wasn't an art major. He certainly did the research, even if he didn't spend his time going to museums and art galleries like Daniel. He had a genuine desire to learn, but Daniel had to admit he'd only just gotten comfortable with him. Yet, that hadn't lasted long.

"It's OK, but we don't really..." Daniel wasn't sure how to explain it. "Maybe it's a personality thing."

"Incompatible?"

Daniel shrugged and said nothing. He felt awfully close to unburdening himself with Dr. Tate. Something about the man made Daniel think he'd be sympathetic, but he wasn't used to opening up to people. He wasn't used to being the one who needed help.

"That's tough. I know a thing or two about dealing with someone who annoys you."

Daniel stared at his sketchbook and saw how some of the pencil marks had blurred. Lines that had been initially sharp and defined, overtime, became fuzzy and light. People were the same way he thought. Confident and sure one moment, wavering and scared the next. Daniel went through those phases all the time. There's no reason that Casey didn't as well.

"Well," the professor added. "The annoying man makes life... less boring? I guess."

Dr. Tate sounded as if he was begrudgingly admitting to

something not entirely clear to Daniel. The man sighed and put his hands deep into his pockets and turned to leave the room. "Stop looking at old sketchbooks and start filling up new ones," he said as he reached the door. He waved and left.

Daniel closed his sketchbook and had to admit Dr. Tate was right. His attention should be on his art, not being pulled around by Casey. Daniel considered the professor's other advice. Did he want a less boring life, he wondered? If anything he could use a more boring life. Life without his heart being pulled in every direction. Maybe boring was what he needed.

He pulled out his phone, his hands shaking, and carefully typed his message.

30

———

Casey skipped his Thursday morning class. It was statistics, a hold out from his business, major, and not something he was particularly passionate about. He slept poorly, and when he woke, he felt sore, as if he'd been pummeled in his sleep. He recognized that he was pummeling himself.

He kept rehashing the night before in his mind, thinking of how he should've acted differently. He should've run after Daniel immediately instead of sitting there, shocked, not knowing what to do. He wished he could blame it on the sheer force of his father's personality, but his influence on Casey had begun to wane when he graduated high school, and he had no one but himself to blame for his inaction.

His manager at the store offered him an extra shift if he could come in immediately, and Casey jumped at the chance to be distracted. The sky was cloudless and a deep blue, and it pissed him off that the weather could be so indifferent to his pain. He kept checking his phone to see if Daniel had contacted him and felt less and less surprised when he hadn't. He left a message in the morning, hoping that maybe they could get together and talk. But what would he say? How would he explain himself?

His boyfriend ran away scared, and he did nothing. Even Casey didn't think he deserved forgiveness.

At work, the manager put him on stocking duty instead of the counter. Thankfully, he didn't have to smile at the customers with his depressive mood, but it was harder to become distracted with mere physical labor. His body also felt broken. He sat on two stacked milk crates in the cooler, taking a break after stocking the milk, and checked his phone one more time. Nothing.

As the day went on the more he thought about what happened the more he started to find explanations for himself. Maybe he was too exhausted to do anything? He'd been working extra hours over the last month trying to get ahead of his bills so that he had some extra money for the holidays. He remembered why he wanted the extra money. He hoped to take Daniel on a short trip away over winter break, just the two of them someplace nice and cozy. At that point, he would present him with his gift. He had imagined the face Daniel would make, wondering if he'd be delighted or embarrassed.

Casey thought it might not be enough, but that it would be the first in a long line of everything that he wanted to give to Daniel. He never felt this way about anyone else before, and it was making it confusing on how to act. His parents had a great relationship and provided a great example of two adults that truly loved each other. But if he were to use them as an example, he would end up putting himself in the place of his father, and the man infuriated him. His father saw Casey as a new version of himself, and Casey wanted so much more.

He took out the empty cartons from the cooler into the back of the store and broke them up for recycling. He never used a box cutter for these, instead he liked punching out the sealed ends with his fist. It made a lot of noise, but it relieved a lot of stress.

His manager found him moments later punching wildly at an empty box of sports drinks and surrounded by the cardboard carcasses of its friends.

"Casey? Anything you wanna talk about?"

Casey shook his head. "I don't think so." He stood there, not reacting, not knowing what more to say, for the last few minutes his head was only focused on punching.

"Casey? How about you head out?"

Casey looked up at the clock in the storeroom wall. "I still have a couple of min—"

"Casey? You're gonna go home now. No. Leave the cardboard, I will take care of it." His voice was kind but firm, and Casey had learned if he had to tell you something twice, it was three times too many.

Casey agreed and stepped carefully over the wreckage. His walk home was just as insulting with the sun high overhead making the early autumn leaves glow with orange and yellow light. The picture of High Street with its small shops and eateries always reminded Casey of a greeting card or painting. It was one of the things that drew families to Woodlawn outside of the college. But, walking down the tree-lined street today made him angry. He couldn't understand why everything was so bright when everything was so wrong.

Riley was home by the time Casey got there, but they only exchanged a few words. As usual, Riley was on his way out as Casey was on his way in, but there seemed to be even more tension between them than before. Casey still didn't fully understand how Riley felt about his relationship with Daniel, though Riley wasn't forthcoming with his feelings even at the best of times. He emptied his duffel bag and placed it on his bed so he could pack for the weekend. Behind him, he heard the door open and then shut. He had assumed that Riley had left until he heard his voice.

"I don't know what to tell you," Riley said in that casual way close friends do as if all their conversations are part of one long conversation.

"I know. I don't even know what to ask." Casey pulled some shirts from a neat stack next to his desk. He shoved them into the duffel bag, not thinking too much about what clothes to bring. Since he was going home, he technically didn't have to pack anything at all.

"I'm no good for this stuff," Riley said. "But I am probably the authority on overthinking. It's never good to just be stuck inside your own head. That's not where the answers are. I guess."

Casey stood over his half-filled duffle bag and smiled. His friend had given him a simple piece of advice, but for some reason, hearing it in Riley's voice made it seem profound. He looked over his shoulder. "You're right. Thanks."

A few seconds later, he heard the door shut and knew Riley had actually left. While Casey finished packing, he thought about what he imagined Daniel needed most. Were he in that position, Casey thought, he would want reassurance and comfort. He'd noticed Daniel's insecurity, and it hurt him that his presence didn't immediately cure that. That was arrogance on his part.

He decided to leave a message on Daniel's voicemail, letting him know he was heading home for the weekend and asking to see him Monday when he got back. He would tell him that he was sorry and that he should've come after him. He'll tell him that he'll never let Daniel doubt him again. He held his phone tightly in his hand.

He might even tell him, what? That he loved him? Casey's heart beat faster. It was true, had always been true. Why not say it?

His phone beeped. It was a text message from Daniel. Casey's hand shook as he touched the screen. And then his stomach filled with lead.

"Casey. I'm sorry. I don't think this will work."

31

Even though he was in his own room, and his own bed, Casey barely slept his first night home. No one was around when he arrived, so he put a note on the kitchen counter and went upstairs to stare at his phone, trying to make it ring once again. Exhaustion took over, and he fell asleep after about ten minutes of vigilance.

He woke to the aroma of fresh coffee and waffles coming up from the kitchen below and realized his mother must be home. He couldn't imagine his father downstairs, a tiny apron wrapped around him, standing there whipping up a batch of batter. Casey imagined the man giving him a sweet smile and asking, "how did you sleep, honey," as he came into the kitchen.

Any other time the image would have made Casey laugh, but today he wondered if he could stay in his room until his inevitable conversation with his father. Since it was only Friday, he had the idea he wouldn't see him until Saturday. His father stayed at one of his hotels during the week. His sudden appearance at Casey's apartment made him think that he must be spending the week in Philadelphia.

Casey stretched and tried to get some of the stiffness out of his shoulders. He must not have moved around enough at night, though he felt as if he was tossing and turning constantly. He didn't have nightmares, or even fully-formed dreams, but just a constant feeling of loss. He was certain he had messed things up completely, even before they had begun.

He heard rapid footsteps outside his door, and before it violently burst open, Casey steeled himself against what was to come.

"Good morning, skid mark!" Casey put up his arms as a defensive posture against his sibling's aura. Alex stood there decked out in denim from head to toe. They wore a denim jacket with a denim shirt underneath, a pair of oversized jeans, and white cowboy boots. The only thing missing was a denim cap, but Casey thought there wasn't a hat big enough to contain the mass of blond hair they'd spun into an old-fashioned style on their head. The last time he'd seen his older sibling in person was a year ago, just as they were heading off to graduate school in Iowa. The whole family thought this would settle them down a bit. Alex strode into the room and pulled Casey out of bed by his feet.

The whole family was mistaken.

"Why are you up here?" Alex asked. Casey was captivated by the sheer engineering of their hairstyle. With all the yelling and tugging, it didn't move at all. "Mom wants you downstairs for breakfast."

Casey's backside landed on the floor, and Alex let go. They squatted down next to him. Alex had inherited their mother's face and kind eyes. It didn't quite mesh with the human tornado that Casey grew up with.

"I'll be down. I'm just not feeling like talking yet this morning."

Alex tilted their head. "It's not like you to be depressed. Have you grown up a bit this past year?"

Casey scowled. "What do you mean grown up?" The question annoyed him, especially coming from this denim demon.

"I mean, normally you're all Casey-Go-Lucky. I could smell the change in your attitude from the other side of the door."

"Is that why you kicked it in?"

Alex nodded furiously. "Yes. Yes. I needed an entrance of emergency proportions." They stood and straightened their jacket. Casey could see small jewels glued in places along the arms. "She said you and Dad are fighting."

Casey sighed, pulled his legs up to his chest and hugged them. Alex had always been a larger than life presence growing up, but they never insisted Casey be someone he wasn't. They wanted to take Casey on adventures, or make him do dangerous things, or on occasion, take blame for something being broken in the house. But when they weren't completely occupied with their own life, Alex was always trying to pull him out of himself. The problem was Alex was eight years older than Casey and just not always around.

"It's not a fight, more as if we have different ideas of who I should be."

Alex waved away the comment. "That's what parents are supposed to do, skiddo. I mean they make the blueprint, and then it's your job to revise it. Capiche?"

Casey screwed up his face and looked at his sibling. "Capiche? Who are you? And what's with the denim?"

Alex's face split into a comic book smile. "I am Alex!"

The siblings stared at each other. And then Casey realized that that's all there was to it.

"And," Alex added. "I'm gonna eat your waffles."

They dramatically turned away from Casey, bent over, and farted—loudly. They ran out the door, slamming it. He heard the running footsteps going down the stairs and a distant admonition from their mother.

Sitting in the stink, Casey laughed. The encounter hadn't necessarily made him feel better, but it certainly made him feel like he was home. And sometimes, that was enough.

After breakfast, Alex left to hang out with friends, and Casey, his stomach full of waffles, joined his mother on the sun porch, where she was reading. To outsiders, his parents seemed like complete opposites: his father was a high achieving businessman, running a string of luxury hotels along the East Coast, and his mother spent her days reading and writing. Considering the small easel and paint tray he saw sitting next to her, Casey assumed she had picked up watercolor painting recently. It immediately made him think of Daniel and how well the two of them would get along.

The morning sun warmed the space as the low wall of plants against the windows brought the outside inside. His mother culti-vated a green thumb carefully over the years. At least twenty different sizes of pots and trays lined the room, with two hanging spider plants taking over the valances with their offspring.

His mother put down her book and patted the place on the wicker sofa next to her. "How did you sleep?"

"Not great," he admitted.

His mother ruffled his hair, and that feeling of being a kid washed over Casey. He didn't mind, and he even considered that maybe that was what he needed. Over the last few months he had been working hard to point himself in one very specific direction, towards Daniel. And he thought it might now all be for nothing. He was feeling a bit lost, and anytime you're lost, it's probably good to head home, at least for a bit.

"Your father and I have been talking about you." She said it like a question as if she was waiting for Casey's response, but all he did was shrug.

"Your father doesn't know how to picture success outside of the road he took."

Casey turned to her, surprised. Often, his mother served as the heart of the family and instead of making the big decisions, held everybody close when they were in pain. She wasn't necessarily the solution, her children needed to find that on their own, but she was always the balm. Her face seemed more stern than usual, some of the softness was gone.

"More importantly," she continued, "your father has always seen himself in you."

"That's the problem," Casey said, pouting. "He's not really seeing me."

"Don't misunderstand," his mother reached out and grabbed his hand. "Your father sees himself in you and that is a great source of pride. Not because you are following him. But because you are amazing on your own, and still, he can see something of himself in that."

Casey didn't misunderstand at all what she was saying. It must've shown on his face because she laughed and continued.

"You know how it is when you think someone is amazing? You just want to be part of that, even just a little?"

Casey immediately thought of Daniel. He thought of the moment he'd seen him and how he'd been pulled toward him all this time. He thought of all the stupid things he did to try to get Daniel's attention and how all it really took was sitting in front of him in class. He thought of how excited he was every time Daniel showed up at practice. He thought of how often he wanted to go talk to him when he saw him around campus. He thought of how he felt in his arms the last time he saw him. He understood what it was like to think someone was amazing.

"It's kind of like that," his mother said. Her face was softer now. She must've thought she was getting through. "He hasn't figured out that you don't have to *be* him in order to be part of him. Your father is smart and successful, but he is a simple man."

The frustration Casey felt was all mixed up, partly over his father, partly over Daniel, and he was starting to realize that he had to work out one of those relationships before he could fix the other. Since he was home, he may as well start with his father. At least he had all day to think about how to start.

His mother patted his knee. "He should be home soon. Since you're here, he's taking Friday off."

Casey turned to his mother whose smile looked so much like Alex's that it unnerved him, and he had some suspicion that more was going on behind those faces than he assumed.

32

Daniel sat on the floor at the coffee table, his back pressed up against the sofa. He pulled out a brand new sketchbook, hoping to distract himself from being depressed. He'd felt hollow in his stomach since the moment he sent the text to Casey. Every hour there wasn't any response made him feel worse. He couldn't imagine Casey quiet or sad, and he hated the idea he may have made him feel that way. It felt like he was blocking the sun, casting a shadow.

And just in case Daniel felt a little too proud to have been able to break someone's heart, he also entertained the idea that Casey didn't care. Maybe he saw the message and thought, "Well, guess it didn't work out," or "Well, let me try someone else." And any number of awful things. Deep down, he felt that would be out of character for Casey. And, as usual, any doubt that Daniel had came strictly from himself, right?

Casey had been physically distant when around other people. Casey hadn't told his friends about them even though they had just started dating. Maybe there was a reason for Daniel to doubt that it wasn't manufactured by his own insecurity. But, no matter what, his insecurity made everything worse.

He stared at the white expanse of an empty page. Then he leaned forward, put his forehead on the slightly rough surface, and groaned.

"I hate myself for saying this, but are you sure you made the right choice?"

Daniel twisted around so he could look up at Jess sitting on the sofa. "I'm surprised to hear that coming from you. You seemed to dislike Casey from the moment I mentioned him."

"My dislike has nothing to do with your relationship, though." Jess crossed his arms and looked away. "As much as it pains me to say this... Is breaking it off the right choice?"

Daniel turned back to his page and its mocking emptiness. "I don't know. But I feel like I'm hurting no matter what I do. At least now I don't have to worry about hurting someone else."

Jess was quiet, and Daniel held his breath, waiting to hear his response. He didn't always get the best advice from Jess, they had different perspectives on the world, so Daniel tried to take things in the spirit in which it was given. But for some reason today, he really wanted to know what he thought. He wasn't sure when he sent the text. He also knew that sending a text to break up was lame, but he knew he couldn't say it to Casey's face.

"You guys have only been dating for a couple of days, and I think there's a lot going on here."

Daniel waited for more, and when it didn't come, he pushed himself up so he could sit on the sofa properly. "That's pretty vague, but yeah I don't know why this feels different. I don't know why I feel so strongly that on the one hand, I want to be with him, but on the other hand, I feel like I can't. Nothing about the world he lives in seems to have a place for me."

Jess sighed. "Maybe you're expecting too much too soon."

Daniel watched his friend struggle. It was almost comical to see Jess suffer through his dislike of Casey to help Daniel. But he appreciated his friend's loyalty. "Do you think I was hasty?"

"No," Jess said, looking up at the ceiling. "I think you were scared."

Jess repositioned himself on the sofa so he could look at Daniel. The two spent plenty of time here watching movies, doing homework, talking, but Daniel couldn't remember having this serious of a conversation. Over the last year they had spent less and less time together, their day-to-day schedules not matching up like they used to. They could have the odd meal together but weren't able to spend any down time together anymore. Daniel was starting to understand how much he missed that and how he had fallen into himself over the past year. What he needed was a friend, and in his own way, that's what Jess had always been.

"Jess, I'm always scared. I don't have your confidence, certainly not your looks. And I feel like I've been untethered since my mom died. I feel like I could float away. I didn't know how much of what I did was for her. I didn't know how much of who I am was because she saw me."

Daniel cried. The tears had been there all along, but he needed something to shake them loose. At that moment, he wasn't ashamed, he was just lonely. And he understood the reason he broke up with Casey wasn't because they were incompatible or that he was scared. But he didn't want to use Casey to cure his loneliness.

He bent forward and sobbed for the first time in a long time. Jess moved closer, putting his hands on Daniel's shoulders, not holding him but letting him know he was there. They stayed like that for a little while, Jess occasionally leaving for tissues and a glass of water. And then just as suddenly as it started, Daniel finally let go.

"I'm always surprised how much crying makes you hungry,"

Daniel said, sniffling and wiping his face. He felt so much better, not healed but better, as if the knot in his stomach unraveled. He was feeling too raw to call Casey, but he promised himself he'd call in the morning. He wanted to see him. He needed to see him and explain. He wanted to take it all back. And he didn't want to hurt him ever again.

The phone buzzed the moment Jess came out of the kitchen, a bowl of tomato soup in each hand. Daniel stared at the screen puzzled.

"Is that Casey?" Jess asked.

"No," Daniel said. "It's a Philadelphia number."

He hit the button, "Hello. Yes, this is Daniel Marsden..."

33

———

AFTER LUNCH, Casey went into the backyard to shoot hoops. Alex had been the basketball player in the family and embarrassed him many times on the half court in the backyard. Granted, he was eight years old to their sixteen, so he barely had a chance. He could attribute a lot of his athleticism to trying to best Alex, even though not once did he ever prevail.

He couldn't help but inventory all the ways he went wrong with Daniel. From the moment they started talking, he tried to imagine what he could've done differently to make Daniel feel more secure or make him feel more confident in his feelings. He only asked him out the other day, but it seemed like he was losing a long-term relationship. Maybe what he was losing was the promise of a relationship. Or that he had told himself this would be his last. He felt there must still be something he could do, but that answer was blocked off from him.

He took a shot when his father suddenly appeared and snagged the rebound. He held a lacrosse stick in his left hand, which he tossed to Casey. "Let's go to the wall." It wasn't a request.

The two men, each with his own stick and gloves, moved to the side of the detached three-car garage behind the house. Along the midpoint of the wall, about 3 feet from the ground, were a series of neon green circles, painted over the years. Casey and his father stopped about 4 feet from the wall and started tossing the ball against it, catching it skillfully as it bounced back.

Thwack. Thwack. Thwack.

"Where's your phone?" His father asked. "I've been texting."

"I left it in my room. It kept not making noise."

Both men switched places, tossing now from their non-dominant hands.

Thwack. Thwack. Thwack.

"The assistant dean called me. That's why I was on campus."

Casey flinched and missed a catch. He retrieved the ball but said nothing.

"He called multiple times, and I couldn't avoid him any longer. He was worried about your sudden change in major."

"It was only sudden to him."

Casey switched to a behind-the-back toss, easily flipping the ball from his stick over his left shoulder. His father mirrored him, though less fluidly.

Thwack. Thwack. Thwack.

"Way back in my day I had him as a professor. I never liked him. Weaselly kind of guy."

Casey laughed, "Yeah, that's him."

The light settled into a golden sheen as they moved into the late afternoon. The nearest neighbor was far enough away that they could only hear them in the weird way winter carries noise across the land. To Casey it seemed they had the whole world to themselves for now.

Thwack. Thwack. Thwack.

"Why sociology?"

"Not sure yet. I want to explore it a bit. Business was definitely not for me." Casey went back to a regular toss. "To be honest, I kinda hated it."

His father stopped his toss. He turned toward Casey and leaned on his stick. "You know now I have to change all of my plans?" His face was stern and serious. Casey felt like shrinking from his gaze but took a deep breath and held this place. As his father continued. "If I'm gonna leave everything to Alex, I'm gonna have to start by reinforcing all the doors."

Casey squinted his eyes, looking at his father, wondering if it was a joke or not. Slowly, a smile crept across his father's face and he realized his father might have just given his blessing. Casey started laughing so hard he dropped his stick into the grass.

"Most definitely," Casey said between laughs. "Most definitely."

His father walked over and slapped Casey on the shoulder but said nothing more. They both picked up their lacrosse sticks and started swinging for the wall again, the tension between them broken.

Thwack. Thwack. Thwack.

"So, about that guy..." his father said.

Casey felt the stick fly out of his hand on the toss, the back end smacking the brick wall. He slouched and stared at the ground. "Ah, well. That's not an issue anymore, I guess."

His father again stopped his own tossing. "Is that okay with you?"

Casey picked up his stick and leaned against the wall. "No, but it wasn't my call."

He looked out across the lawn, avoiding his father's gaze. He didn't want that small feeling of hope to get any bigger just to be disappointed. He wasn't pessimistic, but right now, Casey couldn't see any way back to Daniel.

His father held the lacrosse stick in both hands and raised it over his head, stretching. "Well. You can accept things as they are and move on. Or, you can make a better offer."

Casey frowned. "It's not a business deal, Dad."

"Oh, I disagree." He pointed the stick at Casey's chest. "It's a negotiation, surely. Same thing."

Casey pushed the stick away. "I'm not pressuring him."

His father scoffed. "If you're pressuring, you're *not* negotiating. That's what little men do. And I didn't raise a little man."

Casey raised his chin ready to push back against the comment, but ultimately had to admit his father was right. He wasn't telling Casey to show power but to be confident. He wasn't telling Casey to force Daniel to take him back, but to plead his case once more. His father made him realize that sometimes you fight for what you believe in.

"I'm afraid of scaring him off completely," Casey said.

"Maybe you can't help it. You're the spitting image of your old man, after all." His father smiled, playing it off as a joke, but Casey had to admit he was right. How much of his energy day-to-day was spent being outgoing and happy? Making himself seem less intimidating, more approachable. The golden boy.

Daniel made him want to drop the act. Daniel made him feel possessive. He looked at the imposing figure of his father, essentially a glimpse into his own future, and understood why Daniel broke up with him. Casey was too much.

"I have to be a bastard because of shareholders," his father said. "And that's not always easy to turn off."

He nodded in the direction of the house. "You, though, take after your mother. You've got kindness in you. Lean into that."

He said nothing more. He picked up the lacrosse gear and headed back toward the house.

Casey squatted down and started pulling at the grass, thinking. Within a few moments, his father had approved of everything that mattered in Casey's life. He felt a little sick to his stomach that he'd doubted the man at all. In his own desire to distance himself from his "legacy," he'd neglected the most important thing his father needed: to be a dad.

Casey wondered if he finally got the message. It was time to get out of his own way and make a path back to Daniel. He wasn't even sure how to start.

34

Monday morning brought a little hope for Casey. What it didn't bring was Daniel. Determined to talk to him before class started, Casey waited outside the lecture hall before their modernism class. He thought it would be easier for Daniel to avoid him in the classroom, so he wanted a chance to meet with him first. He didn't want to ambush Daniel, but he wanted a chance to talk.

By the time class was about to start, Casey had lost hope of seeing him that morning. Professor Tate arrived and only noticed Casey sitting there when he had his hand on the door.

"Casey? What are you doing?"

Casey sat on the short wall, taking in as much of the world as he could. No Daniel. "I'm not sure." He barely registered Professor Tate holding open the door. He just didn't feel like moving.

"Is everything OK?" Professor Tate asked.

Casey didn't answer, just slowly got up and walked into the lecture hall. He tried not to slouch as he made his way up the stairs. He waved to Shane and Brett and sat down. He could feel the empty seat behind him, and for the first fifteen minutes of class, he kept his eye on the door, remembering the day, not too long ago, when Daniel ran in breathing heavily, hand on his side. Casey smiled to himself, remembering how cute he'd been. Now, he wasn't there, and every breath threatened to bring tears. He'd never been this sad in his life.

"Mr. Stanfield? Wake up."

Casey wasn't asleep, but he wasn't exactly awake either. He had been looking at his notebook the entire class, scribbling a word here or there, but mostly distracting himself from his own thoughts. Professor Tate stood at the front of an empty lecture hall.

"Sorry," Casey stood up and gathered his things. "I guess I zoned out a bit."

"That seems to be going around," Tate said.

Casey had a sense of being examined as he came down the stairs towards the front. The professor followed him over to the door and stopped him before he left.

"I'm not gonna say this isn't like you," Tate said. "But, is there something I can help with?"

Casey just looked forward towards the doors, wanting to get outside and start his search. He didn't want to meet Professor Tate's eyes because he had a feeling he would explain everything. He had spent the summer taking supplementary classes from this man, and outside of the classroom, he might consider Professor Tate a friend. But he didn't know what kind of help this friend could give him, and so he just shook his head and said, "Thanks." He moved quickly to the outside doors and left.

It wasn't like him, he knew, or was this the first time he let himself be something other than, what did Alex call him? Casey-Go-Lucky.

He wasn't sure how long they were gonna let him sit at the window seat in the café without buying anything, but Riley didn't give him a chance to find out. He didn't even notice when Riley walked by trying to get his attention until his roommate came inside and actually tapped him on the shoulder. "What are you doing here?"

"Hoping to find an answer to all my problems."

Riley stood there for a moment, saying nothing. Students trickled in and out of the café, but the quad outside was deserted. It had been an unusually wet September, and today promised to be no different. It matched Casey's mood, as if the sky was telling him that he had no chance with Daniel. Don't bother.

"Well," Riley said. "There's only one solution to all the world's problems."

Casey looked up at him just as Riley looked down and said. "Let's go lift."

Casey caught himself almost bursting out laughing at the ridiculousness of the suggestion. But something about it made perfect sense. Instead of engaging his mind, he needed to engage his muscles to the point of exhaustion, so he didn't have to feel like this anymore. He had lost all momentum when Daniel didn't show up for class. What he needed was to burn that negativity out of him. Casey stood up with his things and followed Riley across the grass.

Casey tried to stay positive, but he carried his gloom into the training area. A number of his teammates were already working out and talking. Shane and Hiro were doing free weights by the mirror, while Kellen and Brett seem to be racing each other on the rowing machines, neither saying a word. Casey watched them for a moment. It was the quietest rivalry he had ever witnessed.

Casey sat down on a bench but made no move to change into his sweats. He heard the clank of free weights being put back in the rack.

"Holy shit. Casey, what's wrong? You get dumped?" Shane said.

It was no use hiding. "Yeah."

Hiro sat next to him on the bench. "The artist? Aww, I liked him."

Casey nodded. "So do I."

It took a minute for Casey to realize the weight room had gone quiet. Even the whirring of the rowing machines stopped. He looked up to see all of his teammates staring at him in surprise. He was about to explain when Shane spoke for the group.

"Wait, you're gay?"

Casey shrugged. "I don't think so?"

"Then bi? Or, what's that word?" Shane pointed. "Hiro..."

Hiro sat straight up. "Why me?"

Shane ignored him. "Bi-curious?"

Casey hung his head, already tired of the conversation. "I don't know."

"You don't know?" Shane moved closer, his hands on his hips. "Man, that's some hefty privilege weighing you down. No wonder you're depressed."

"Hey," Riley said.

"Nah, man," Shane continued. "Look. I don't care who you like, but you're all happy-go-lucky dude, and you get depressed when you fall for a guy?"

Shane's face showed genuine annoyance, and Casey felt a little defensive.

"That's cold," Shane said.

Riley tried to defend his friend. "He's depressed because—"

"I'm depressed because he doesn't trust me."

Shane huffed. "Not used to *not* being the golden boy, eh?"

Brett chimed in from the rowing machine. "Dude. What the hell?"

But Shane waved him off and stayed focused on Casey. "You think maybe you should walk away?"

He felt annoyed. Shane had an aggravating way of seeing the

truth while still playing the idiot. In the end, all Casey could do was be honest. "Everywhere I walk leads to him."

No one said a word. Casey realized he had brought the whole group down with his problems and guilt added itself to the bundle of feelings swirling in his chest.

Shane clapped him on his shoulder. "Look, buddy, there's not a lot a bunch of boneheads like us can do, but we're here for you."

"You were just giving him shit," Brett said, moving over toward the group.

"No more shit than I normally give him," Shane replied. "You gotta get out of your own head sometimes."

"Shane," Riley said, "you should probably spend more time in your own head once in a while." He selected a couple of dumb-bells from the rack. "You need to keep an eye on whatever's going on in there."

"Yeah," Hiro said, jumping into the conversation. "And stop picking on me."

Casey smiled as the room erupted into bickering. He caught snippets of insults, and feigned offense, but for the most part, he was just happy that he had found support and acceptance by this group of guys. He was a little ashamed he didn't come to them in the first place. He'd never doubt them again.

Kellen sat down next to him. He wasn't sure what to expect from the freshman; he rarely spoke unless he was complaining about Hiro. He looked at Casey as if he wanted to say something but was afraid.

"You can say whatever you want." Casey offered.

"I think it's important to say clearly how you feel." Kellen said. "I could see that he liked you, but I couldn't see that you two had started dating"

Casey stared at the freshman and understanding filled in his brain. He knew he was taking it slow, but he thought that was because Daniel seemed cautious, skittish. He didn't want to scare him away by bringing him into his life wholeheartedly. But maybe, Casey thought, that that's exactly what he should've done. What he should've done was an overwhelming expression of confidence in their relationship.

"That would probably be a big deal for him," Kellen continued. He looked down at his own hands. "No one likes to be a secret."

Casey finally got it. He could've hugged the kid but settled for a nice long squeeze of his shoulder. He headed for the door, then turned back. "Kellen! No laps for you until spring."

The last thing Casey heard as he sprinted away was Hiro, whining. "Awww. No fair!"

35

CASEY SPENT an hour walking around the residential areas near the campus. He had a vague notion where Daniel's apartment was but didn't have an exact address. He found an area he thought was right, and there were two apartment buildings next to each other. He wasn't sure what to do next. Casey stood on the sidewalk and stared from one to the other, willing Daniel to appear. He seriously considered knocking on every door until he found him. He would probably be arrested.

An expensive sedan pulled into the lot where he was standing, and a man that looked vaguely familiar got out. He seemed to recognize Casey but walked away from him. But before he got to the stairs of the building, he turned around and came back.

"He's not here." The man stood there with his hands in his pocket, as if that was all he had to say.

"What? Who are you?" Casey asked. He couldn't place the man, but thought he had seen him on campus, or maybe he had a class with him at some point. Either way it didn't matter, this wasn't who he was looking for.

"Looking for Daniel, right? He's gone."

Heat spread through Casey's chest a mix of worry and anger. "Where is he and, again, who are you?"

The man's phone rang, and he turned away from Casey to take the call. He spoke quickly in a different language, Italian maybe. Casey's impatience got the better of him, which only made him more confused.

The man ended the call and without looking at Casey said, "Go home—"

Without thinking, Casey took three steps forward, unsure of his next move. "Who the fuck are you?"

The man stood his ground. "I'm Daniel's roommate, Jess, and the one telling you to leave."

Casey forgot Daniel had his own roommate. He'd imagined the roommate to be someone like Daniel, quiet, small, non-threatening, but this guy was the same size as Casey, maybe an inch taller, and he had to admit, good looking. Knowing that this guy lived in the same apartment as Daniel turned his confusion into the beginnings of jealousy.

"Where is he?" Casey said, trying to keep himself calm.

Jess tilted his head and said calmly. "Look, why don't you just leave him alone."

Casey stepped forward, fighting against the urge to grab the guy by the collar. Frustration coursed through him and while he didn't like this guy at all, he needed to find Daniel. The fact that he wouldn't tell Casey outright meant something was wrong.

Jess leaned his head back and looked down at him. "Not used to getting rejected?"

Casey moved closer, squaring his shoulders and pulling every ounce of his father into his being. It had an effect and Jess took a step backward. He was tired of people treating him as if he was some spoiled, rich kid. He was shaking, not used to this level of anger coursing through him.

"Tell me."

The smirk left Jess's face and he seemed to shrink. "Franklin," he said abruptly. "He's at Franklin."

Casey didn't understand. "What? Franklin what?" He took another step closer, the last one.

Jess brought his hands up to hold him back. "Franklin Hospital in Philly for fuck's sake."

Casey felt his heart sink and his thoughts narrowed into a pinpoint focus. Without a second glance, he ran out of the parking lot and down the street. He didn't ask why Daniel would be at the hospital, but he decided that he wanted to see for himself. He had a feeling he wasn't getting any more information out of the roommate.

Casey headed through the tree-lined street. People dotted the sidewalks, moving in and out of shops. He easily dodged around them, at one-point hurdling over a suitcase sitting outside the pub. A few shouts followed him, but he was around the corner before most of the shoppers noticed.

Casey ran as hard as he could, hoping that Riley was home. He was going to need the car.

36

———

DANIEL HAD ARRIVED the day before, and his father hadn't yet gone into surgery. He was still in Franklin Hospital's emergency room and they hadn't cleaned off all of the blood. When a nurse saw him standing at the edge of the room, she took him gently back outside to let him know that his father looked much worse than he actually was. The car had rolled into an embankment, but his father had been securely fastened into the seatbelt. It saved him from being thrown out of the car.

The nurse called to one of the EMTs that had brought his father in. He didn't have all of the details, but it looked like his father tried to avoid hitting a deer. Route 12 was a winding, dark road, but one that his family often took on the way out to Maryland. Rich enjoyed driving that road, he often said that Pennsylvania had some of the best winding roads in the country.

When the police called and said he was in a car accident, Daniel worried that his father had been drinking again. He had never driven drunk, but he wasn't sure if his father's recent uptick in mood would signal a drastic downtick later on. He felt ashamed that he automatically thought his father had done this to himself, but Daniel was relieved to be wrong.

Richard had a broken femur and three broken ribs. A tree branch punctured the windshield on the passenger side. Broken glass caused quite a few lacerations on his face and arms.

"That's where all the blood came from," the EMT told him. "He'll look better once he's all cleaned up."

Sitting next to him after surgery, Daniel had to admit he did look better. He had scratches all over but his skin looked healthy, not the pale, sickly tone he'd been since the funeral. He had a black eye, but the lines on his forehead seemed to have smoothed out. The doctor assured him the surgery went fine, and that while he was facing a long stretch of rehabilitation, he should be "right as rain, eventually."

Daniel took a deep breath and relaxed for the first time in what seemed like forever. He squeezed his father's hand. "I'll be right back, Dad."

Daniel leaned back in the waiting room chair and sighed. He winced as something poked his hip. Sudden realization made him pull out his phone for the first time in hours. He'd never even thought to check it since everything truly important was right in front of him. Almost everything, he thought, then wondered if there would be any message from Casey. He'd decided that he rushed his decision to break up. Did they even have anything to break up anyway?

He hit the side button, his gut clenching in anticipation of what, nothing? Anything? He wasn't sure. It didn't matter anyway. His battery was dead.

"Shit."

Daniel found an outlet and plugged in, but his phone was ancient, and it would take a while to get enough juice to check his messages. He sat on the floor and pulled out his sketchbook and a random pencil.

He moved the pencil across the paper, mostly for the soft sounds of scratching than with any visual intent. He let the last line inform the next, trying to get his upper brain out of the way as Dr. Yang would tell him. Art, any art, she lectured, was not the product but the practice, and the practice was largely about opening a channel between your subconscious and your implement or tool. For him it was the pencil, or charcoal, or paint brush —though the pencil was his favorite. For some it was the keyboard or the voice. Dr. Yang's practicum mentored students from many disciplines and even some outside of the art department altogether. Her methods and reputation were well-known across campus. So, Daniel let his pencil do the work.

From under the chair his phone beeped. He looked up and bent forward to check the screen when it beeped again. And again. And again. Even in the empty waiting room, Daniel scrambled to grab the phone and silence it, not wanting to disturb anyone else. He parked his pencil behind his ear and lay down on the carpet. The screen came to life.

"Oh no," he said. He saw Casey's phone number in the missed call list, a small number "10" next to the listing. There were only seven voicemails, and Daniel wondered if he'd given up. But the phone kept beeping, receiving the text messages that had been sent an hour ago, then 45 minutes ago, then 30, then ten.

"Where are you?"

"Are you alright?"

"Seriously you have to tell me, at least are you ok?"

"Your roommate is a dick and you better be ok"

"Please please please pick up the phone"

"PLEASE"

Daniels' stomach fluttered and sank, like an anchored butterfly. He was worried that Casey was upset but so happy that he still cared. The mixed-up feelings left him confused, and his fingers hovered over the call-back button. What would he even say? How could he start to explain? But more importantly, was he too late?

The phone rang in his hand and he dropped it. It was Casey.

"Hello?" Daniel said, cringing.

"I'm in the lobby but they won't let me in!"

Daniel was taken aback. "What lobby? Where?"

Casey sounded winded. "I'm at the hospital lobby, but they won't let me in. I'm not family so I'm stuck here."

"Why are you here?"

Casey shouted. "What do you mean 'why am I here?' Why are *you* here? Are you alright?"

Daniel had no idea how Casey found him. "How did you know—"

"Your asshole roommate said you were at the hospital. So, *I'm* at the hospital."

Daniel closed his eyes and saw Jess's smirking face in his mind. "Dammit. I'm alright. It's my dad. My dad was in an accident."

He could hear Casey let out a long sigh. He was silent for a while, then said, "Is your dad alright?" Daniel could hear his voice quivering.

"Yeah, he's going to be fine. It's alright."

They sat on the phone in silence for another moment. Daniel wanted to thank him and tell him he could head home. He felt bad that Casey made the trip under a misunderstanding, even if that misunderstanding was probably intentional. But somehow, he felt a little happy, too.

"You're gonna have to do it," Casey said.

"What?" Daniel thought he'd missed something.

"They won't let me in. I'm not family. I'm not anything. Security won't let me in. I wanted to make this grand entrance and come to your bedside, but I'm stuck."

Daniel sat up. "But I'm not hurt. I just told you—"

"You're gonna have to come get me." Casey said

Daniel lost track of the conversation. Everything he'd been doing over the last twenty-four hours had been focused on getting his father well. Now he was being asked to come rescue *this guy*.

"I don't understand what you want—"

Casey shouted. "I am here for YOU, but I can't get there. It's up to you, now."

Daniel waited, his heart racing.

"COME GET ME!" Casey yelled and hung up.

Daniel jumped to his feet and ran into the hallway, the pencil falling from behind his ear and onto the floor.

37

THE SECURITY GUARD stood with his arms folded and a stern look on his face as Daniel tried to explain. Casey stood behind him as if being protected and it made Daniel's heart race to have Casey so close. He was still out of breath from racing down the hallway. The guard calmly reminded him that running in hospital hallways was frowned upon, and Daniel promised never to do it again.

"I don't want to hear about you two making a lot of noise," the security guard said. He looked at Daniel and then at Casey. He lingered on Casey as if it was the source of all of his problems that evening. Daniel couldn't help but relate, as Casey was the source of some of his own.

He waited while Casey got a visitor tag from reception. As they left, Casey grabbed Daniel's hand as they walked slowly and quietly toward the elevators. A couple of nurses followed them into the elevator, chatting.

Casey whispered, "How is he doing?"

"He's doing better but he's sleeping right now." Daniel couldn't keep his voice from shaking. The lack of sleep and worry had depleted his energy. Casey moved closer to him and he suddenly felt overwhelmed by this man and the display of - there was nothing else to call it - love.

"Have you slept," Casey asked.

"Not really. I was just gonna crash in the waiting room."

The elevator stopped on the third floor and the nurses moved aside as Daniel and Casey exited. The waiting area was just off the main hallway behind a pair of automatic sliding glass doors. The room was lined with comfortable chairs and a small play area at the far end loaded up with picture books and puzzles. Daniel had been alone there most of the night.

Casey walked straight for the chair with Daniel's bag and sat down in front of it. He sat crossed-legged and smiled up at Daniel. He slapped his thigh. "Put your head here and get some rest."

"What?" Daniel said, not really understanding.

"Your head here," Casey pointed at Daniel then at his leg. "I can be your pillow. Get some rest. I'll stay here." He waved his hand for Daniel. "I'll wake you if they need you."

Daniel did as he was told and awkwardly lay down. He was grateful, but had to admit it wasn't all that comfortable.

Casey brought his face close and smiled. "I don't often skip leg day," he said. "My bad."

Daniel laughed. "I guess not." He turned to face the doors and shifted his body. As soon as he closed his eyes, the exhaustion washed over him. His final thought before falling asleep was how he wished he'd had someone like this the last time he rushed to the hospital. Not just someone, he thought, feeling a hand on his back. Casey. He wished he'd had Casey.

38

Four months earlier.

Casey knew the shower wouldn't make him feel better and the constant noise coming from his teammates was giving him a headache. The bus ride back from New Jersey had been quiet., Their coach let them sit in their own disappointment instead of rehashing what went wrong during the game. It was the first time Woodlawn had gotten to the semifinals in a generation. In fact, it was Casey's father that had led the team to their first league championship. It wasn't lost on him that part of his disappointment was not living up to his father's expectations. But also, he just really wanted to win.

Shane had been inconsolable once they hit the locker room. He missed a couple of key passes in the last half and no amount of reassurance from Riley or Doug could calm him down. They had played their hardest. They just weren't good enough this time. It's just how it was.

It didn't mean it didn't hurt.

He left the locker room and started walking aimlessly around the quad until he ended up outside the student union building.

People were coming and going through the main entrance, and he wandered in for distraction and out of curiosity as to what was going on. Final exams had ended a week ago and more than students were milling about. A sign in the lobby announced the Woodlawn Annual Art Show and a round of applause drew him into the main room. Most of the people stood in the center of the hall, and on the stage they faced stood a single painting. As soon as Casey saw it, his heart skipped a beat.

The canvas was mostly white. There were dots of teal and navy blue sprinkled around it. The figure was leaping, their legs bent. Their arms held a lacrosse stick and were extended across the chest, readying a pass. The helmet blocked the player's face, but the tufts of hair curling out underneath the back and the shape of the shoulders gave Casey chills. He wasn't conceited, no matter what other people said, but he would've put money down that that was a picture of him, leaping and readying for a toss.

He moved closer, trying to get a better look. He couldn't take his eyes off how realistic the fabric looked, but also how stylized the whole figure was. Casey didn't have the vocabulary to describe what he was seeing. Business majors rarely take art classes. The number on the jersey was distorted by the creases in the shirt. It could have been a six or a sixteen. Casey wore a six. He immediately decided that he would always wear a six.

There were two people on the stage near the painting: an older man that Casey didn't recognize and the younger one with dark hair and a soft face. He assumed he was a student and probably the artist, but he looked frightened and a little bit lost. Casey understood that face and that feeling. He'd felt it walking off the field only hours before. What he didn't understand was the other feeling that was growing inside him, and why he couldn't take his eyes off the dark-haired artist.

The older man said something to the artists, and the artist said "Thank you." He was presented with a certificate and an envelope. A man standing next to Casey said, "I'm surprised a sports picture won first place at Woodlawn," and he didn't understand what would be unusual about it. The artist was obviously talented, and whether he was the subject of the painting or not, Casey thought it was the best damn painting he'd ever seen. He wanted to run up on stage and shake that guy's hand. He felt like he'd been transported into a different world altogether.

Was it because he had painted Casey in such a way that made him feel seen? He always saw his father's face when he walked around campus. He always saw his father's school, but this painting with the obscured jersey front with his masked face showed only Casey. Even if he only wanted to see himself in the portrait after a tough loss, what he saw was *his* body, *his* movement, in what he could absolutely guarantee was *his* moment of pure joy. Somehow, that guy on the stage had caught that.

That guy on the stage had caught Casey.

He tried to move closer to the stage, but the attendees pushed him back. He ended up following a couple of patrons as they headed toward a large display table. They would be auctioning off the paintings later that afternoon, even the prize-winner. Casey decided he had to win. He grabbed a pamphlet that listed all the artists in the show and found his guy: Daniel Marsden.

Daniel. Daniel. Daniel, he thought. Daniel Marsden. That's the name. That's the name he had to remember.

All thoughts of the league championship disappeared as he searched for Daniel in the dwindling crowd. He circled the conference room twice but never found him.

But he had a name, and if he played his cards right, he would soon have a painting.

Now, all he needed was a plan.

$$39$$

FOUR MONTHS EARLIER.

Daniel still wasn't sure why he was on the stage and kept thinking it had been all a mistake. The last four months had been full of darkness as far as his art was concerned. When his mother received her diagnosis, he felt numb and distant from his work. He would still occasionally try to sketch people around campus to keep up the practice, but he was only trying to avoid the fact that he was losing his mother.

They had talked about it over winter break. His mother was kind and part of that kindness meant being honest. The three of them spent those weeks watching movies, playing games, reading, but mostly just talking. She was home when Daniel returned to school. She went back into the hospital in February and had been there ever since.

She and his father both insisted that he go to the art show. Dr. Yang had submitted one of his pieces without his knowledge. He was furious at first, but she explained to him that the painting he had done deserved to be seen. Even though everything he was doing now felt dark and was an expression of his pain, he had still produced a moment of happiness. Dr. Yang believed very much that people should be exposed to happiness, especially in times of pain, and he consented to the entry.

Now he was winning first prize and having to stand in front of all of the attendees and smile. The outgoing president of the college handed him a certificate that had his name on it. He didn't care; he grimaced, nodded, and bowed at the clapping for his painting. It came out of a sketch of someone he saw running around campus all the time. He was drawn to the man and therefore started drawing him in return. When he captured the jump, he had been sitting inside the student union looking out the window onto the practice fields. He never felt comfortable getting too close to his subjects, in case somebody would think he was weird. Unfortunately, Daniel was used to people thinking he was weird.

The fact that it had translated so beautifully to the impressions of color and movement without detailed lines, surprised even Daniel. If asked, Daniel would be hard pressed to remember the whole process and sometimes felt like it was done in a fugue state. The only thing he was sure about was that it made him uneasy to see it. He hid it in the practical art room because he didn't think he had a right to feel good about it. It wasn't fair to his mother to be happy.

When Dr. Yang found it, she said the world should see it. "If not the world," she had said, "then Woodlawn."

The talking and clapping had died down, and people were milling about. He felt like he could breathe again, and he moved to the edge of the stage to make his escape. The phone in his back pocket buzzed. It was his father, and he was a little excited to tell him he'd won first place in the show.

"Hey Dad." Daniel said.

There was silence on the other end of the call, and then his father caught his breath and said, "Danny, I'm sorry, but I think you need to get to the hospital right now."

Daniel ran and made it just in time.

40

PRESENT TIME.

They sat together in the waiting room, squeezed into one of the wider chairs. Casey had his arms around Daniel and had decided not to let him go until he absolutely had to. The floor-to-ceiling glass walls before them looked out onto the nurses' station. It was still too early in the morning for a lot of activity, but occasionally a nurse would walk by and smile.

"I'm sorry you had to be alone that day. I wish I'd known you already so I could've been there," Casey said, and he pulled Daniel closer trying to show physically what he meant in words. He wanted Daniel to know he would never have to be alone again.

"It wouldn't have been good anyway." Daniel said, leaning his head on Casey's shoulder and squeezing his hand. "Dad and I went to a pretty dark place at first. I think we were blaming ourselves. We had taken it for granted she'd always be around."

Casey felt Daniel's breath brush against his cheek, and he turned to see him looking up at him. It was the same blue eyes that he'd seen across the room during the show. He couldn't believe he was looking into them now.

Daniel smiled. "You got here eventually though"

Casey wondered how his own family would weather the loss of one or both of his parents. His father would be inconsolable if something happened to his mom. There was no doubt of the man's love for her, and he thought he might talk to the old man about not taking her for granted. Casey assumed that Alex would show up and take over, as was their personality. But sitting here with Daniel, he realized that it was less about Alex and more about not expecting much from himself.

Casey leaned his head back against the wall, starting to feel the exhaustion of the last few days. He'd have to leave soon. Riley would need his car back for work, but he wanted to stay here as long as possible.

"I think I'll go back home this weekend and give my mom a hug." Casey said.

Daniel laughed and nuzzled his head back against Casey's shoulder. The fragrance of Daniel's shampoo had faded, and all Casey could smell was a light sweat and the solvent used by the floor cleaners. But he breathed it all in, securing the moment in his memory and connecting it to this feeling. Perhaps, when he came back to visit Daniel's father, he would think about this moment what he'd almost lost, and what he most certainly had gained.

"Depending on how your dad's doing, I want you to come with me one weekend. You should meet her. She gives the best hugs"

Daniel didn't move and almost seemed to be holding his breath. He pulled away so he could see Daniel's face and noticed that tears were falling down his cheeks, but he was smiling. "I guess that's where you get it from," Daniel said.

Daniel sat up and threw his arms around Casey's neck, pulling him close for a kiss. Casey fell into him easily, returning the kiss with an urgency of his own. They held each other for a while, before the wall of glass, for all the world to see.

EPILOGUE

"You have been begging him to draw you all semester. Now stand still!"

Hiro was practically vibrating as he stood in the practical room holding the long stick across his shoulders. His right leg was bent with his foot resting upon a cinderblock to keep him in a particular pose. Kellen stood next to him, still as a statue, holding his short stick before him, no expression on his face. Until Hiro whined, and then he would glare at his teammate.

"How long?" Hiro said. "You can sketch so fast at practice."

Daniel tried his best to keep his pencil on the paper while not giggling. "This sketch has to be a little more detailed since it's going to be a painting, eventually. "

It had been Casey's idea to come up with his punishment when the two freshmen had been caught fighting in the locker room, again. Daniel agreed easily to the task. He thought it would make a fun addition to his work, but also be a chance to get to know some of Casey's teammates a little better.

Casey, on the other hand, didn't seem as interested in the freshman. The moment he arrived in the practical room, he had pulled a stool over to where Daniel sat, slid it right behind him and wrapped his arms around Daniel's waist. He'd asked Casey if anything was wrong, and his boyfriend replied, "Nope. This is where I sit while you do this."

He'd only returned to the practical room to empty out his art locker. He wanted to make sure he had all of his sketch books at home so he could work on unfinished pieces and select his next paintings from the collection. Also, his father was eager to see his new work and enjoyed flipping through Daniel's sketchbooks in the rehabilitation hospital.

At first, Daniel had struggled to move his arms while Casey hugged him, but he decided to enjoy the warmth in the usually cold practical room. There was no question that the two were dating now, and Daniel had been surprised to discover how clingy Casey could be. He wondered if he was making up for lost time. They even walked hand-in-hand into the administration building when Daniel went to apply for a semester's leave. It meant he would graduate late, but it also meant he got to spend one more semester on campus with Casey.

Casey peeked over Daniel's shoulder toward the two models. "I'm just here to make sure you guys behave. My presence is all that's necessary."

Daniel felt Casey's lips brush his neck, and he dropped his pencil. "How much longer," Casey whispered in his ear.

"I can stop anytime. It's your idea to make them stand still." He tried to bend down to get his pencil, but Casey had a strong hold on him.

"Hey!" Hiro shouted. "Will you paint us like this?"

Hiro had moved to the edge of the room toward a canvas leaning against the wall. It was the painting of Casey entered into the annual contest, and Daniel had been surprised to see it here when he'd arrived. If the artist allowed, the top ten paintings went into a silent auction with the proceeds benefiting scholarships for the art department. Since Daniel hadn't even considered entering the contest in the first place, he agreed to the auction. His artwork had felt useless at the time. He never expected to see the painting again.

"No," Casey answered. "No one gets painted like that ever."

Daniel twisted away from Casey's grasp to see him pouting. It wasn't just the need to always be touching Daniel, but there was a child-like possessive streak in him, too. He narrowed his eyes and scowled. "You don't get to say how I paint." He tried to sound playful but the sentiment was sincere.

Casey seemed to get the message. He addressed the players. "Your painting will be different," and he paused to think. "Because you're different types of player." Casey looked back at Daniel who nodded.

"See," Casey continued, letting Daniel go and stretching. He approached Hiro and Kellen, who had joined his teammate by the painting. "This is less about lacrosse and more about jumping." He pointed to the legs of the painting, his legs. "I used to jump hurdles, so this is more about my skills than the game."

Daniel marveled at the display of salesmanship. Casey pointed to the area where the freshmen were supposed to be modeling. "You two are exemplary versions of the model lacrosse player. You don't need to be in an action pose because your bodies exude that wound up energy that explodes on the field."

Hiro's eyes grew wide and Daniel believed that any admiration he already felt toward Casey must have tripled in that moment. Kellen's typically stoic exterior seemed to crack when he smiled.

"So," Casey said, leading the two back to the cinderblocks. "You two stand here. Stand still. And let yourself be sketched while I have cuddle time with my boyfriend."

Hiro and Kellen both opened their mouths to say something, but thought better and moved back to the modeling area.

Casey returned to his stool and to wrapping his arms around Daniel, who laughed. He half turned his head, still unable to see Casey because he was so close. "You are so spoiled."

"I get that a lot," Casey said. His voice muffled as his face pressed up against Daniel's shoulder. "Spoil me more."

ABOUT THE AUTHOR

Hartlee Finn lives in the Mid-Atlantic area of the United States and has the accent to prove it. While not writing about idiots in love, she thinks about how she *should be writing* while playing Stardew Valley and helping students write their college essays.

For more information about Hartlee and to get updates on the next book in the Woodlawn College Series, sign up for her newsletter at hartleefinn.com

WHAT ABOUT RILEY?

Riley Cross has more problems than just his idiot roommate, Casey.

When a strange guy in a suit crosses his path on the first day of classes, Riley has to find a way to navigate the man's interest while also keeping up with his school work, his job, and the sudden responsibility of being *de facto* captain of the lacrosse team.

Subscribe to get notified for the preorder.
Expected release date: May 15th, 2026

ALSO BY HARTLEE FINN

The Woodlawn College Romance Series

Art History

Lacrossed Lovers

Book 3 coming soon!